ANCESTRAL
VOICES

MORE WILDSIDE CLASSICS

Please see www.wildsidepress.com for a complete list!

ANCESTRAL VOICES

An Anthology
of
Early Science FIction

Edited by

R. Reginald
and
Douglas Melville

WILDSIDE PRESS

ANCESTRAL VOICES

This edition published in 2006 by Wildside Press, LLC.
www.wildsidepress.com

CONTENTS

A Glance Ahead

BEING A CHRISTMAS TALE OF A.D. 3568

JUST how it came about, or how he came to get so far ahead, Dawson never knew, but the details are, after all, unimportant. It is what happened, and not how it happened, that concerns us. Suffice it to say that as he waked up that Christmas morning, Dawson became conscious of a great change in himself. He had gone to bed the night before worn in body and weary in spirit. Things had not gone particularly well with him through the year. Business had been unwontedly dull, and his efforts to augment his income by an occasional operation on the Street had brought about precisely the reverse of that for which he had hoped. This morning, however, all seemed right again. His troubles had in some way become mere memories of a remote past. So far from feeling bodily fatigue, which had been a pressingly insistent sensation of his waking moments of late, he experienced a startling sense of absolute freedom from all physical limitation whatsoever. The room in which he slept seemed also to have changed. The pictures on the walls were not only not the same pictures that had been there when he had gone to bed the night before, but appeared, even as he watched them, to change in color and in composition, to represent real action rather than a mere semblance thereof.

"Humph!" he muttered, as a lithograph copy of "The Angelus" before him went through a process of enlivenment wherein the bell actually did ring, the peasants bowing their heads as in duty bound, and then resuming their work again. "I feel like a bird, but I must be a trifle woozy. I never saw pictures behave that way before." Then he tried to stretch himself, and observed, with a feeling of mingled astonishment and alarm, that he had nothing to stretch with. He had no legs, no arms—no body at all. He was about to

A Glance Ahead

indulge in an ejaculation of dismay, but
there was no time for it, for, even as he began, a terrifying sound, as of rushing
horses, over his bed attracted his attention.
Investigation showed that this was caused
by an engraving of Gérôme's "Chariot
Race," which hung on the wall above his
pillow—an engraving which held the same
peculiar attributes that had astonished
him in the marvellous lithograph of "The
Angelus" opposite. The thing itself was
actually happening up there. The horses
and chariots would appear in the perspec-
tive rushing madly along the course, and
then, reaching the limits of the frame,
would disappear, apparently into thin air,
amid the shoutings and clamorings of the
pictured populace. Three times it looked
as if a mass of horseflesh, chariots, chari-
oteers, and dust would be precipitated upon
the bed, and if Dawson could have found
his head there is no doubt whatever that he
would have ducked it.

"I must get out of this," he cried. "But,"
he added, as his mind reverted to his disembodied condition, "how the deuce can I?
What 'll I get out with?"

"Over the Plum-Pudding"

The answer was instant. By the mere exercise of the impulse to be elsewhere the wish was gratified, and Dawson found himself opposite the bureau which stood at the far end of the room.

"Wonder how I look without a body?" he thought, as he ranged his faculties before the glass. But the mirror was of no assistance in the settlement of this problem, for, now that Dawson was mere consciousness only, the mirror gave back no evidence of his material existence.

"This is awful!" he moaned, as he turned and twisted his mind in a mad effort to imagine how he looked. "Where in thunder can I have left myself?"

As he spoke the door opened, and a man having the semblance of a valet entered.

"Good-morning, Mr. Dawson," said the valet—for that is what the intruder was—busying himself about the room. "I hope you find yourself well this morning?"

"I can't find myself at all this morning!" retorted Dawson. "What the devil does this mean? Where's my body?"

"Which one, sir?" the valet inquired, respectfully, pausing in his work.

" ' GOOD-MORNING, MR. DAWSON ' "

A Glance Ahead

"Which one?" echoed Dawson. "Wh— which— Oh, Lord! Excuse me, but how many bodies do I happen to have?" he added.

"Five—though a gentleman of your position, sir, ought to have at least ten, if I may make so bold as to speak, sir," said the valet. "Your golf body is pretty well used up, sir, you've played so many holes with it; and I really think you need a new one for evening wear, sir. The one you got from London is rather shabby, don't you think? It can't digest the simplest kind of a dinner, sir."

"The one I got from London, eh?" said Dawson. "I got a body in London, did I? And where's the one I got in Paris?" he demanded, sarcastically.

"You gave that to the coachman, sir," replied the valet. "It never fitted you, and, as you said yourself, it was rather gaudy, sir."

"Oh—I said that, did I? It was one of these loud, assertive, noisy bodies, eh?"

"Yes, sir, extremely so. None of your friends liked you in it, sir," said the valet. "Shall I fetch your lounging body, or will

you wish to go to church this morning?"
he continued.

"Bring 'em all in; bring every blessed
bone of 'em," said Dawson. "I want to
see how I look in 'em all; and bring me a
morning paper."

"A what, sir?" asked the valet, apparently somewhat perplexed by the order.

"A morning paper, you idiot!" retorted
Dawson, growing angry at the question.
The man seemed to be so very stupid.

"I don't quite understand what you wish,
sir," said the valet, apologetically.

"Oh, you don't, eh?" said Dawson,
amazed as well as annoyed at the man's
seeming lack of sense. "Well, I want to
read the news—"

"Ah! Excuse me, Mr. Dawson," said
the valet. "I did not understand. You
want the *Daily Ticker*."

"Oh, do I?" ejaculated Dawson. "Well,
if you know what I want better than I do,
bring me what you think I want, and add
to it a cup of coffee and a roll."

"I beg your pardon!" the valet returned.

"A cup of coffee and a roll!" roared Dawson. "Don't you know what a cup of

coffee and a roll is or are? Just ask the cook, will you—"

"Ask the what, sir?" asked the valet, very respectfully.

"The cook! the cook! the cook!" screamed Dawson. His patience was exhausted by such manifest dulness.

"I—I'm sincerely anxious to please you, Mr. Dawson," said his man; "but really, sir, you speak so strangely this morning, I hardly know what to do. I—"

"Can't you understand that I'm hungry?" demanded Dawson.

"Oh!" said the valet. "Hungry, of course; yes, you should be at this time in the morning; but—er—your bodies have already been refreshed, sir; I have attended to all that as usual."

"Ah! You've attended to all that, eh? And I've breakfasted, have I?"

"Your bodies have all been fed, sir," said the valet.

"Never mind me, then," said Dawson. "Bring in those well-fed figures of mine, and let me look at 'em. Meanwhile, turn on the—er—*Daily Ticker.*"

The valet bowed, walked across the

room, and touched a button on a board which had escaped Dawson's vigilant eye —possibly because his vigilant eye was elsewhere—and, with a sigh of perplexity, left the room. The response to the button pressure was immediate. A clicking as of a stock-ticker began to make itself heard, and from one corner of the bureau a strip of paper tape covered with letters of one kind and another emerged. Dawson watched it unfold for a moment, and then, approaching it, took in the types that were printed upon it. In an instant he understood a portion of the situation at least, although he did not wholly comprehend it. The date was December 25, 3568. He had gone to bed on Christmas eve, 1898. What had become of the intervening years he knew not—but this was undoubtedly the year of grace 3568, if the ticker was to be believed—and tickers rarely lie, as most stock-speculators know. Instead of living in the nineteenth century, Dawson had in some wise leaped forward into the thirty-sixth.

"Great Scott!" he cried. "Where have I been all this time? I don't wonder my poor old body is gone!"

A Glance Ahead

And then he started to peruse the news. The first item was a statement of governmental intent. It read something like a court circular.

"It is pleasant to announce on Christmas morning," he read, "that the business of the Administration has proven so successful during the year that all loyal citizens, on and after January 1, will be paid $10,000 a month instead of only $7600, as hitherto. The United States Railway Department, under the management of our distinguished Secretary of Railways, Mr. Hankinson Rawley, shows a profit of $750,-000,000,000 for the year. Mr. Johnneymaker, Secretary of Groceries, estimates the profits of his department at $600,000,000,-000, and the Secretary of War announces that the three highly successful series of battles between France and Germany held at the Madison Square Garden have netted the Treasury over $500,000 apiece — no doubt due to the fact that Emperor Bismarck XXXVII. and King Dreyfus XLVIII. led their troops in person. The showing of the Navy Department is quite as good. The good business sense of Secretary Smithers in securing the naval fights between Russia and the Anglo-Indians for American waters is fully established by the results. The twenty encounters between his Indo-Britannic Majesty's Arctic squadron and the Czar's Baltic fleet in Boston Harbor alone have cleared for our citizens $150,000,000 above the guarantees to the two belligerents; whereas the bombardment of St. Petersburg by the Anglo-Indians under our management, thanks to the efficient service of the Cook excursion-steamers direct to the scene of action, has brought us in several hundred millions more. It should be quite evident by this time that the Barnum & Bailey party have shown themselves worthy of the people's confidence."

Dawson forgot all about his possible bodily complications in reading this. Here was the United States gone into business, and instead of levying taxes was actually paying dividends. It was magnificent.

One might have thought that the unexpected announcement of the possession of an income of $120,000 a year would be sufficient to destroy any interest in whatever

A Glance Ahead

other news the *Ticker* might present; but with Dawson it only served to whet his curiosity, and he read on:

"The acquirement of the department stores by the government in 2433 has proven a decided success. Floorwalker-General Barker announces that the last of the bonds given in payment for the good-will of these institutions have matured and been paid off. This, too, out of the profits of four centuries. It is true that the laws requiring citizens to patronize these have helped much to bring about this desirable effect, and some credit for the present wholly satisfactory condition of affairs should be given to Senator Barca di Cinchona, of Peru, for having, in 2830, introduced the bill which for the time being covered him with execration. The profits for the coming year, on a conservative estimate, cannot be less than eighteen trillions of dollars—which, as our readers can see, will add much to the prosperity of the nation."

"Worse and worse!" cried Dawson. "Floorwalker-General—compulsory custom—eighteen trillions of dollars!" And then he read again:

"Over the Plum-Pudding"

"It will be with unexpected pleasure this Christmas morning, too, that our citizens will read the President's proclamation, in view of the unexampled prosperity of the past year, ordering a bonus of $15,000 gold to be delivered to every family in the land as a Christmas present from the Administration. This will relieve the vaults of the national Treasury of a store of coin that has been somewhat embarrassing to handle. The delivery-wagons will start on their rounds at six o'clock, and it is expected that by midday the money will have been wholly distributed. Residents of large cities are requested not to keep the carriers waiting at the door, since, as will be readily understood, the delivery of so much coin to so many millions of people is not an easy task. It is suggested that barrels of attested capacity be left on the walk, so that the coin may be placed into these without unnecessary delay. Those who still retain the old-fashioned coal-chutes can have the gold dumped into their cellars direct if they will simply have the covers to the coal-holes removed."

Dawson could hardly believe the announcement. Here was $15,000 coming to him this very morning. It was too good to be true, he thought; but the news was soon confirmed by the valet, who interrupted his reading by bursting breathlessly into the room.

"What on earth are we going to do, Mr. Dawson?" he cried. "The Christmas present has arrived. The cart is outside now."

"Do?" retorted Dawson. "Do? Why, get a shovel and shovel it in. What else?"

"That's easier said than done, sir," said the valet. "The gold-bin is chock-full already. You couldn't get a two-cent piece into the cellar, much less three thousand five-dollar gold pieces. They'd ought to have sent that money in certified checks."

Dawson experienced a sensation of mirth. The idea of quarrelling as to the form of a $15,000 gift struck him as being humorous.

"Isn't there any place but the gold-bin you can put it in?" he demanded. "How about the silver-bin, is that full?"

"I don't know what you mean by the silver-bin," replied the valet. "People don't use silver for money nowadays, sir."

"Over the Plum-Pudding"

"Oh, they don't, eh? And what do they do with it—pave streets?"

The valet smiled.

"You are having your little joke with me this morning, Mr. Dawson," he said, "or else you have forgotten that all we do with silver now is to make it into bricks and build houses with 'em."

"Well, I'll be hanged!" cried Dawson. "Really?"

"Certainly, sir," observed the valet. "You must remember how silver gradually cheapened and cheapened until finally it ruined the clay-brick industry?"

"Ah, yes," said Dawson. "I had temporarily forgotten. I do remember the tendency of silver to cheapen, but the ruin of the brick industry has escaped me. This house is—ah—built of silver bricks?"

"Of course it is, Mr. Dawson. As if you didn't know!" said the valet, with a deprecatory smirk.

"Ah—about how much coal—I mean gold—have we in the cellar?" Dawson asked.

"In eagles we have $230,000, sir, but I think there's half a million in fivers. I haven't counted up the $20 pieces for eight weeks, but I think we have a couple of tons left, sir."

"Then, James— Is your name James?"

"Yes, sir—James, or whatever else you please, sir," said the valet, accommodatingly.

"Then, James, if I have all that ready cash in the cellar, you can have the $15,000 that has just come. I—ah—I don't think I shall need it to-day," said Dawson, in a lordly fashion.

"Me, sir?" said James. "Thank you, sir, but really I have no place to put it. I don't know what to do with what I have already on hand."

"Then give it to the poor," said Dawson, desperately.

Again the valet smiled. He evidently thought his master very queer this morning.

"There ain't any poor any more, sir," he said.

"No poor?" cried Dawson.

"Of course not," said James. "Really, Mr. Dawson, you seem to have forgotten a great deal. Don't you remember how the forty-seventh amendment to the Constitution abolished poverty?"

"I—ah—I am afraid, James," said Dawson, gasping for breath, "that I've had a stroke of some kind during the night. All these things of which you speak seem—er—seem a little strange to me, James. There seems to be some lesion in my brain somewhere. Tell me about—er—how things are. Am I still in the United States?"

"Yes, sir, you are still in the United States."

"And the United States is bounded on the north by—"

"Sir, the United States has no northerly or southerly boundary. The Western Hemisphere is now the United States."

"And Europe?"

"Europe has not changed much since 1900, sir. Don't you remember how in the early years of the twentieth century the whole Eastern Hemisphere became European?"

"I remember that we took part in the division of China," said Dawson.

"Oh yes," said James, "quite so. But in 1920 don't you recall how we swapped

A Glance Ahead

off our share in China, together with the
Dewey Islands, for Canada and all other
British possessions on this side of the
earth?"

"Dimly, James, only dimly," said Dawson, astonished, as well he might be, at
the news, since he had never even imagined anything of the kind, although the
Dewey Islands needed no explanation.
"And we have ultimately acquired the
whole hemisphere?"

"Yes, sir," replied James. "The South
American republics came in naturally in
1940, and the Mexican War in 2363 ended,
as it had to, in the conquest of Mexico."

"And, tell me, what are we doing with
Patagonia?"

"One of the most flourishing States in
the Union, Mr. Dawson. It was made the
Immigrant State, sir. All persons immi-
grating to the United States, by an act of
Congress passed in 2480, were compelled to
go to Patagonia first, and forced to live
there for a period of five years, studying
American conditions, after which, provided
they could pass an examination showing
themselves equal to the duties of citizen-

ship, they were permitted to go wherever else in the States they might choose."

"And suppose they couldn't pass?" Dawson asked.

"They had to stay in Patagonia until they could," said James. "It is known as the School of Instruction of the States. It is also our penal colony. Instead of prisons, we have a section of Patagonia set apart for the criminal element."

"And the negro?" asked Dawson. "How about him?"

"The negro, Mr. Dawson, if the histories say rightly, was an awful problem for a great many years. He had so many good points and so many bad that no one knew exactly what to do about him. Finally the sixty-third amendment was passed, ordering his deportation to Africa. It seemed like a hardship at first, but in 2863 he pulled himself together, and to-day has a continent of his own. Africa is his, and when nations are at war together they hire their troops from Africa. They make splendid soldiers, you know."

"What's become of Krüger and—er— Rhodes?" Dawson asked. "Turned black?"

A Glance Ahead

James laughed. "Oh, Rhodes and Krüger! Why, as I remember it, they smashed each other. But that is ancient history, Mr. Dawson."

"Jove!" cried Dawson. "What changes!" And then an idea crossed his mind. "James," said he, "pack up my luggage. We'll go to London."

"Where?" asked James.

"To the British capital," returned Dawson.

"Very well, sir," said James. "I will buy return tickets for Calcutta at once, sir. Shall we go on the 1.10 or the 3.40? The 1.10 is an express, but the 3.40 has a buffet."

"Which is the quicker?" Dawson asked.

"The 3.40 goes through in thirty-five minutes, sir. The 1.10 does it in half an hour."

"Great Scott!" said Dawson. "I think, on the whole, James, I won't try it until to-morrow. Calcutta, eh!" he added to himself. "James," he continued, "when did Calcutta become the British capital?"

"In 2964, sir," said James.

"And London?" queried Dawson.

"I don't know much about those island

123

towns, sir," said James. "It's said that London was once the British capital, but sensible people don't believe it much. Why, it hasn't more than twenty million inhabitants, mostly tailors."

"And how many citizens does a modern city have to have, to amount to anything, James?" asked Dawson, faintly.

"Well," said James scratching his head reflectively, "one hundred and sixty or two hundred millions, according to the last census."

"And New York reaches to where?" Dawson asked, in a tentative manner.

"Oh, not very far. It's only third, you know, in population. The last town annexed was Buffalo. The trouble with New York is that it has reached the limits of the State on every side. We'd make it bigger if we could, but Pennsylvania and Ohio and New Jersey won't give up an inch; and Canada is very jealous of her old boundaries."

"Wisely," said Dawson. And then he chose to be sarcastic. "Why don't they fill in the ocean with ashes and extend the city over the Atlantic, James? In an age

"THREE VILLANOUS-LOOKING BODIES, AND A FOURTH, WHICH
DAWSON RECOGNIZED AS HIS OWN"

of such marvellous growth so much waste space should be utilized," he said.

"Oh, it is," returned the valet. "You, of course, know that all the West Indies are now connected by means of a cinder-track with the mainland?"

"And is the bicycle-path to the Azores built yet?" demanded Dawson, dryly.

"No, Mr. Dawson," replied James. "That was given up in 2947, when the patent balloon tires were invented, by means of which wheelmen can scorch wherever they choose to through space, irrespective of roads."

Dawson gasped. "For Heaven's sake, James," he cried, "I need air! Bring up the bodies, and let me get aboard one of 'em and take a sleigh-ride in Central Park. I can't stand this much longer."

The valet laughed heartily.

"Sleigh-rides have gone out in the Central Park, sir. When Mr. Bunkerton started his earth-heating-and-cooling plant snow was practically abolished hereabouts, Mr. Dawson," said he. "It's never cold enough for snow — always about seventy degrees."

"Over the Plum-Pudding"

"Ah! The earth is heated from a central station, eh?" asked Dawson.

"Heated and cooled, sir. What with the hot and cold air running through flues from Vesuvius and the north pole into a central reservoir, an absolute mean temperature that never varies from one year's end to another has been obtained. If you wish to take a sleigh-ride you'll have to go to Mars, sir, and just at present the ships running both ways are crowded. They always are during the holiday season. I doubt if you could secure passage for a week."

"Bring up the bodies!" roared Dawson. "I can't express myself in this disembodied state. Mean temperature everywhere; income provided by government; no taxes; no poor; gold dumped into the cellar; houses built of silver; sleigh-riding at Mars. *Bring up the bodies!* Do you hear? The mere idea is wrecking my mind. Give me something physical, and give it to me quick."

Dawson's emotion was so overpowering that the valet was really frightened, and he fled below, whence he shortly reappeared, pushing before him a small wheeling vehicle in which sat three villanous-looking bodies, and a fourth, which Dawson, with a gasp of relief, recognized as his own.

"I thought you said I had five of these things?" he demanded, inspecting the bodies.

"So you have, sir. The one you wear for evening, sir, is being pressed. You fell asleep in it the other night, sir, and got it all wrinkled."

"That golf fellow's a gay-looking prig!" laughed Dawson. "Let me try him on."

The valet stood the body up, and, opening a small door at the top of the skull, ingeniously concealed by the hair, invited Dawson to enter. Without even knowing how it came about, Dawson soon found himself in full possession. Then he walked over to the glass and peered in at himself.

"Humph!" he said. "Not much to look at, am I? Bring me a driver."

James obeyed, and Dawson tried the swing.

"Why, the darned thing's left-handed!" he said, after some awkward work. "I don't like that."

"You picked it out for yourself, sir," replied the valet. "You said a left-handed player always rattled the other man, and, besides, it was the only one you ever had that could keep its eye on the ball."

"Let me out! Let me out!" screamed Dawson. "I don't like it, and I won't have it. I'm suffocating. Open my head and let me out."

The valet unfastened the little door, and Dawson emerged. "What's that tough-looking one for?" he asked, after a pause, during which his brain throbbed with the excitement of his novel experience.

"Prize-fights," said James.

"And the strange-looking thing that appears to have been designed for a fancy-dress ball?"

"Nobody knows what you intended that for, Mr. Dawson. You had it sent up yourself from the bodydasher's last week, sir."

"Well, take it away," roared Dawson. "This may be 3568, but I haven't lost my self-respect entirely. Give it to—ah—give it to the children to play with."

"Really, Mr. Dawson," said the valet, anxiously, "wouldn't I better ring up the President and have him send a doctor here from the Department of Physic? You

A Glance Ahead

seem all astray this morning. There aren't any children any more, sir."

"Wha — what? No *children?*" cried Dawson.

"They were abolished three centuries ago, sir," explained the valet.

"Then how the deuce is the world populated?" demanded Dawson.

"It was sufficiently populated at the time the law abolishing children was passed, sir."

"But people die, don't they?"

"Never," replied the valet. "When Dr. Perkinbloom discovered how to separate man's mental from his physical side, by means of this little door in the cranium, all the perishable portions of man were done away with, which is how it is, sir, that, for convenience' sake, after the world was as full of consciousness as it could be comfortably, it was decided not to have any more of it."

"But these bodies, James—these bodies?"

"Oh, they are manufactured—"

"But how?"

"That, sir, is the secret of the inventor," replied the valet, "a secret which he is permitted by our government to retain, although the factories are maintained under the supervision of the Tailor-General."

Dawson was silent. He was absolutely overpowered by the revelation.

" James," he said, after a pause of nearly five minutes, "let me—let me back into my old self just for a moment, please. I—I feel faint, and sort of uncomfortable. I feel lost, don't you know. I can grasp some of your ideas, but—Christmas without children! It does not seem possible."

The valet respectfully raised up the original Dawson, opened the little door in the top of its head, and Dawson slipped in.

"Now lock that door," said Dawson, quickly, once he was safe inside. The valet obeyed nervously.

"Give me the key," said Dawson. "Quick!"

"Yes, sir," said James, handing it over, eying his master anxiously meanwhile.

Dawson looked at it. It was a fragile bit of gold, but gold did not appeal to him at the moment, and before the valet could interfere to stop him he had hurled it far out of the window into the busy street below, where it was lost in the maze of traffic.

"There," said Dawson; "I guess you'll have a hard time getting me out of this again. You needn't try. And meanwhile, James, you can kick those other bodies out into the street and dump the gold into the river; after which you may present my compliments to your darned old government, and tell it that it can go where the woodbine twineth. A government that abolishes children can go hang, so far as I am concerned."

James sprang towards Dawson as if he had been stung. His face grew white with wrath.

"Sir," he hissed, passionately, "the words that you have spoken are treason, and merit punishment."

"What's that?" cried Dawson, wrathfully.

"Treason is what I said," retorted the valet, aroused. "If I thought you were in your right mind and knew what you were saying, I should conduct you forthwith to the police-station and inform against you to the Secretary of Justice."

"Over the Plum-Pudding"

"Get out of here, you—you—you impertinent ass!" cried Dawson. "Leave the room! I—I—I discharge you! You forget your position!"

"It is you who forget your position," returned the valet. "Discharge me! I like that. You might just as well try to discharge the President of the United States as me."

Here the valet gave a scornful laugh, and leered maddeningly at Dawson. The latter gazed at him coldly.

"You are my servant?" he demanded.

"By government appointment, at your service," replied James, with a satirical bow. "You have overlooked the fact that the government since 1900 has gradually absorbed all business—every function of labor is now governmental—and a man who arbitrarily bounces a cook, as the ancients used to put it, strikes at the administration. Charges may be preferred against a servant, but he cannot be deprived of his office except upon the report of a committee to the Department of Intelligence. As the President is your servant, so am I."

A Glance Ahead

Dawson sat down aghast, and clutched his forehead with his hands.

"But," he cried, jumping to his feet, "that is intolerable. The logic of the thing makes you, while your party is in power—"

"Your governor," interrupted the valet. "Come," he added, firmly. "You called me an impertinent ass a moment ago, and my patience is exhausted. I shall inform against you. If you aren't sent to Patagonia before night, my name is not James Wilkins."

He laid his hand on Dawson's shoulder roughly. A shock, as of electricity, went through Dawson's person. His old-time strength returned to him, and, turning viciously upon the impudent fellow, he grasped him about his middle with both arms, and, after a struggle that lasted several minutes, dragged him to the window and hurled him, even as he had the key, down into the street below.

This done, he fell unconscious to the floor.

A year has passed since the episode, and Dawson has become the happiest man in

the world, for on his return to consciousness, instead of finding himself in the hands
of a revengeful valet, backed by a social-
istic government, the past had been restored
to him and the future relegated to its proper
place. It was only the other night that he
spoke of the value of his experience, however.

"It has made me happier, in spite of my
many troubles," he said. "If there's anything that can make the present endurable
it is the thought of what the future may
have in store for us. A guaranteed income, and a detachable spirit, and no taxes,
and a variety of imperishable bodies are all
very nice, but servants with the manners of
custom-house officials, and children abolished! No, thank you. Curious dream,
though," he added, "don't you think?"

"No," said I, "not very. It strikes me
as a reasonable forecast of what is likely
to be if things keep on as they are going.
Especially in that matter of our servants."

"Maybe it wasn't a dream," said Dawson. "Maybe, time having neither beginning nor ending, the future is, and I
stumbled into it."

134

A Glance Ahead

"Maybe so," said I. "I think, however, you'll have some difficulty in finding that $15,000 again."

"I don't want to," observed Dawson. "For don't you see I'd find James Wilkins's dead body beside it, and, in spite of its drawbacks, I prefer life in New York to the possibility of Patagonia."

THE THIRD EYE

ALTHOUGH the man's back was turned toward me, I was uncomfortably conscious that he was watching me. How he could possibly be watching me while I stood directly behind him, I did not ask myself; yet, nevertheless, instinct warned me that I was being inspected; that somehow or other the man was staring at me as steadily as though he and I had been face to face and his faded, sea-green eyes were focussed upon me.

It was an odd sensation which persisted in spite of logic, and of which I could not rid myself. Yet the little waitress did not seem to share it. Perhaps she

was not under his glassy inspection. But then, of course, I
could not be either.

No doubt the nervous ten-
sion incident to the expedition
was making me supersensitive
and even morbid.

Our sail-boat rode the shal-
low torquoise-tinted waters at anchor, rocking gently just off the snowy coral reef on which we were
now camping. The youthful waitress who, for economy's sake, wore her cap, apron, collar and cuffs
over her dainty print dress, was seated by the signal
fire writing in her diary. Sometimes she thoughtfully touched her pencil point with the tip of her
tongue; sometimes she replenished the fire from a
pile of dead mangrove branches heaped up on the
coral reef beside her. Whatever she did she accomplished gracefully.

As for the man, Grue, his back remained turned
toward us both and he continued, apparently, to scan
the horizon for the sail which we all expected. And
all the time I could not rid myself of the unpleasant
idea that somehow or other he was looking at me,

watching attentively the expression of my features and noting my every movement.

The smoke of our fire blew wide across leagues of shallow, sparkling water, or, when the wind veered, whirled back into our faces across the reef, curling and eddying among the standing mangroves like fog drifting.

Seated there near the fire, from time to time I swept the horizon with my marine glasses; but there was no sign of Kemper; no sail broke the far sweep of sky and water; nothing moved out there save when a wild duck took wing amid the dark raft of its companions to circle low above the ocean and settle at random, invisible again except when, at intervals, its white breast flashed in the sunshine.

Meanwhile the waitress had ceased to write in her diary and now sat with the closed book on her knees and her pencil resting against her lips, gazing thoughtfuly at the back of Grue's head.

It was a ratty head of straight black hair, and looked greasy. The rest of him struck me as equally unkempt and dingy—a youngish man, lean, deeply bitten by the sun of the semi-tropics to a mahogany hue, and unusually hairy.

5

I don't mind a brawny, hairy man, but the hair on Grue's arms and chest was a rusty red, and like a chimpanzee's in texture, and sometimes a wildly absurd idea possessed me that the man needed it when he went about in the palm forests without his clothes.

But he was only a "poor white"—a "cracker" recruited from one of the reefs near Pelican Light, where he lived alone by fishing and selling his fish to the hotels at Heliatrope City. The sail-boat was his; he figured as our official guide on this expedition—an expedition which already had begun to worry me a great deal.

For it was, perhaps, the wildest goose chase and the most absurdly hopeless enterprise ever undertaken in the interest of science by the Bronx Park authorities.

Nothing is more dreaded by scientists than ridicule; and it was in spite of this terror of ridicule that I summoned sufficient courage to organize an exploring party and start out in search of something so extraordinary, so hitherto unheard of, that I had not dared reveal to Kemper by letter the object of my quest.

6

No, I did not care to commit myself to writing just yet; I had merely sent Kemper a letter to join me on Sting-ray Key.

He telegraphed me from Tampa that he would join me at the rendezvous; and I started directly from Bronx Park for Heliatrope City; arrived there in three days; found the waitress all ready to start with me; inquired about a guide and discovered the man Grue in his hut off Pelican Light; made my bargain with him; and set sail for Sting-ray Key, the most excited and the most nervous young man who ever had dared disaster in the sacred cause of science.

Everything was now at stake, my honour, reputation, career, fortune. For, as chief of the Anthropological Field Survey Department of the great Bronx Park Zoölogical Society, I was perfectly aware that no scientific reputation can survive ridicule.

Nevertheless, the die had been cast, the Rubicon crossed in a sail-boat containing one beachcombing cracker, one hotel waitress, a pile of camping kit and special utensils, and myself!

How was I going to tell Kemper? How was I

going to confess to him that I was staking my reputation as an anthropologist upon a letter or two and
a personal interview with a young girl—a waitress
at the Hotel Gardenia in Heliatrope City?

I lowered my sea-glasses and glanced sideways at
the waitress. She was still chewing the end of her
pencil, reflectively.

She was a pretty girl, one Evelyn Grey, and had
been a country school-teacher in Massachusetts until her health broke.

Florida was what she required; but that healing
climate was possible to her only if she could find
there a self-supporting position.

Also she had nourished an ambition for a post-
graduate education, with further aspirations to a
Government appointment in the Smithsonian Institute.

All very worthy, no doubt—in fact, particularly
commendable because the wages she saved as waitress in a Florida hotel during the winter were her
only means of support while studying for college
examinations during the summer in Boston, where
she lived.

8

Yet, although she was an inmate of Massachusetts, her face and figure would have ornamented any light-opera stage. I never looked at her but I thought so; and her cuffs and apron merely accentuated the delusion. Such ankles are seldom seen when the curtain rises after the overture. Odd that frivolous thoughts could flit through an intellect dedicated only to science!

The man, Grue, had not stirred from his survey of the Atlantic Ocean. He had a somewhat disturbing capacity for remaining motionless—like a stealthy and predatory bird which depends on immobility for agressive and defensive existence.

The sea-wind fluttered his cotton shirt and trousers and the tattered brim of his straw hat. And always I felt as though he were watching me out of the back of his ratty head, through the ravelled straw brim that sagged over his neck.

The pretty waitress had now chewed the end of her pencil to a satisfactory pulp, and she was writing again in her diary, very intently, so that my cautious touch on her arm seemed to startle her.

Meeting her inquiring eyes I said in a low voice:

9

"I am not sure why, but I don't seem to care very much for that man, Grue. Do you?"

She glanced at the water's edge, where Grue stood, immovable, his back still turned to us.

"I never liked him," she said under her breath.

"Why?" I asked cautiously.

She merely shrugged her shoulders. She did it gracefully.

I said:

"Have you any particular reason for disliking him?"

"He's dirty."

"He *looks* dirty, yet every day he goes into the sea and swims about. He ought to be clean enough."

She thought for a moment, then:

"He seems, somehow, to be fundamentally unclean—I don't mean that he doesn't wash himself. But there are certain sorts of animals and birds and other creatures from which one instinctively shrinks —not, perhaps, because they are materially unclean——"

"I understand," I said. After a silence I added: "Well, there's no chance now of sending him back,

"Climbing about among the mangroves above the
water."

even if I were inclined to do so. He appears to be familiar with these latitudes. I don't suppose we could find a better man for our purpose. Do you?"

"No. He was a sponge fisher once, I believe."

"Did he tell you so?"

"No. But yesterday, when you took the boat and cruised to the south, I sat writing here and keeping up the fire. And I saw Grue climbing about among the mangroves over the water in a most uncanny way; and two snake-birds sat watching him, and they never moved.

"He didn't seem to see them; his back was toward them. And then, all at once, he leaped backward at them where they sat on a mangrove, and he got one of them by the neck——"

"What!"

The girl nodded.

"By the neck," she repeated, "and down they went into the water. And what do you suppose happened?"

"I can't imagine," said I with a grimace.

"Well, Grue went under, still clutching the squirming, flapping bird; and he *stayed* under."

"Stayed under the *water?*"

"Yes, longer than any sponge diver I ever heard of. And I was becoming frightened when the bloody bubbles and feathers began to come up——"

"*What* was he doing under water?"

"He must have been tearing the bird to pieces. Oh, it was quite unpleasant, I assure you, Mr. Smith. And when he came up and looked at me out of those very vitreous eyes he resembled something horridly amphibious. . . . And I felt rather sick and dizzy."

"He's got to stop that sort of thing!" I said angrily. "Snake-birds are harmless and I won't have him killing them in that barbarous fashion. I've warned him already to let birds alone. I don't know how he catches them or why he kills them. But he seems to have a mania for doing it——"

I was interrupted by Grue's soft and rather pleasant voice from the water's edge, announcing a sail on the horizon. He did not turn when speaking.

The next moment I made out the sail and focussed my glasses on it.

"It's Professor Kemper," I announced presently.

"I'm so glad," remarked Evelyn Grey.

I don't know why it should have suddenly occurred to me, apropos of nothing, that Billy Kemper was unusually handsome. Or why I should
have turned and looked at the pretty waitress—
except that she was, perhaps, worth gazing upon
from a purely non-scientific point of view. In fact,
to a man not entirely absorbed in scientific research
and not passionately and irrevocably wedded to his
profession, her violet-blue eyes and rather sweet
mouth might have proved disturbing.

As I was thinking about this she looked up at
me and smiled.

"It's a good thing," I thought to myself, "that
I am irrevocably wedded to my profession." And
I gazed fixedly across the Atlantic Ocean.

There was scarcely sufficient breeze of a steady
character to bring Kemper to Sting-ray Key; but
he got out his sweeps when I hailed him and came
in at a lively clip, anchoring alongside of our boat
and leaping ashore with that unnecessary dash and
abandon which women find pleasing.

Glancing sideways at my waitress through my

spectacles, I found her looking into a small hand mirror and patting her hair with one slim and sun-tanned hand.

When Professor Kemper landed on the coral he shot a curious look at Grue, and then came striding across the reef to me.

"Hello, Smithy!" he said, holding out his hand. "Here I am, you see! Now what's up——"

Just then Evelyn Grey got up from her seat be-side the fire; and Kemper turned and gazed at her with every symptom of unfeigned approbation.

I introduced him. Evelyn Grey seemed a trifle indifferent. A good-looking man doesn't last long with a clever woman. I smiled to myself, polish-ing my spectacles gleefully. Yet, I had no idea why I was smiling.

We three people turned and walked toward the comb of the reef. A solitary palm represented the island's vegetation, except, of course, for the water-growing mangroves.

I asked Miss Grey to precede us and wait for us under the palm; and she went forward in that light-footed way of hers which, to any non-scientific man, might have been a trifle disturbing. It had no effect upon me.   Besides, I was looking at Grue, who had gone to the fire and was evidently preparing to fry our evening meal of fish and rice.   I didn't like to have him cook, but I wasn't going to do it myself; and my pretty waitress didn't know how to cook anything more complicated than beans. We had no beans.

Kemper said to me:

"Why on earth did you bring a waitress?"

"Not to wait on table," I replied, amused.   "I'll explain her later.   Meanwhile, I merely want to say that you need not remain with this expedition if you don't want to.   It's optional with you."

"That's a funny thing to say!"

"No, not funny; sad.   The truth is that if I fail I'll be driven into obscurity by the ridicule of my brother scientists the world over.   I had to tell them at the Bronx what I was going after.   Every man connected with the society attempted to dissuade me, saying that the whole thing was absurd and that my reputation would suffer if I engaged in such a ridiculous quest.   So when you hear what that girl and I are after out here in the semitropics, and when you are in possession of the only

evidence I have to justify my credulity, if you want
to go home, go. Because I don't wish to risk *your*
reputation as a scientist unless you choose to risk
it yourself."

He regarded me curiously, then his eyes strayed
toward the palm-tree which Evelyn Grey was now
approaching.

"All right," he said briefly, "let's hear what's up."

So we moved forward to rejoin the girl, who had
already seated herself under the tree.

She looked very attractive in her neat cuffs, tiny
cap, and pink print gown, as we approached her.

"Why does she dress that way?" asked Kemper,
uneasily.

"Economy. She desires to use up the habili-
ments of a service which there will be no necessity
for her to reënter if this expedition proves succes-
ful."

"Oh. But Smithy——"

"What?"

"Was it—moral—to bring a waitress?"

"Perfectly," I replied sharply. "Science knows
no sex!"

"I don't understand how a waitress can be scientific," he muttered, "and there seems to be no question about her possessing plenty of sex——"

"If that girl's conclusions are warranted," I interrupted coldly, "she is a most intelligent and clever person. *I* think they are warranted. If you don't, you may go home as soon as you like."

I glanced at him; he was smiling at her with that strained politeness which alters the natural expression of men in the imminence of a conversation with a new and pretty woman.

I often wonder what particular combination of facial muscles are brought into play when that politely receptive expression transforms the normal and masculine features into a fixed simper.

When Kemper and I had seated ourselves, I calmly cut short the small talk in which he was already indulging, and to which, I am sorry to say, my pretty waitress was beginning to respond. I had scarcely thought it of her—but that's neither here nor there—and I invited her to recapitulate the circumstances which had resulted in our present foregathering here on this strip of coral in the Atlantic Ocean.

She did so very modestly and without embarrassment, stating the case and reviewing the evidence so clearly and so simply that I could see how every word she uttered was not only amazing but also convincing Kemper.

When she had ended he asked a few questions very seriously:

"Granted," he said, "that the pituitary gland represents what we assume it represents, how much faith is to be placed in the testimony of a Seminole Indian?"

"A Seminole Indian," she replied, "has seldom or never been known to lie. And where a whole tribe testify alike the truth of what they assert can not be questioned."

"How did you make them talk? They are a sullen, suspicious people, haughty, uncommunicative, seldom even replying to an ordinary question from a white man."

"They consider me one of them."

"Why?" he asked in surprise.

"I'll tell you why. It came about through a mere accident. I was waitress at the hotel; it happened to be my afternoon off; so I went down to the coquina dock to study. I study in my leisure moments, because I wish to fit myself for a college examination."

Her charming face became serious; she picked up the hem of her apron and continued to pleat it slowly and with precision as she talked:

"There was a Seminole named Tiger-tail sitting there, his feet dangling above his moored canoe, evidently waiting for the tide to turn before he went out to spear crayfish. I merely noticed he was sitting there in the sunshine, that's all. And then I opened my mythology book and turned to the story of Argus, on which I was reading up.

"And this is what happened: there was a picture of the death of Argus, facing the printed page which I was reading—the well-known picture where Juno is holding the head of the decapitated monster —and I had read scarcely a dozen words in the book before the Seminole beside me leaned over and placed his forefinger squarely upon the head of Argus.

" 'Who?' he demanded.

"I looked around good-humoredly and was surprised at the evident excitement of the Indian. They're not excitable, you know.

" 'That,' said I, 'is a Greek gentleman named 'Argus.' I suppose he thought I meant a Minorcan, for he nodded. Then, without further comment, he placed his finger on Juno.

" '*Who?*' he inquired emphatically.

"I said flippantly: 'Oh, that's only my aunt, Juno.'

" 'Aunty of you?'

" 'Yes.'

" 'She kill 'um Three-eye?'

"Argus had been depicted with three eyes.

" 'Yes,' I said, 'my Aunt Juno had Argus killed.'

" 'Why kill 'um?'

" 'Well, Aunty needed his eyes to set in the tails of the peacocks which drew her automobile. So when they cut off the head of Argus my aunt had the eyes taken out; and that's a picture of how she set them into the peacock.'

" 'Aunty of *you?*' he repeated.

" 'Certainly,' I said gravely; 'I am a direct descendant of the Goddess of Wisdom. That's why I'm always studying when you see me down on the dock here.'

" '*You Seminole!*' he said emphatically.

" 'Seminole,' I repeated, puzzled.

" 'You Seminole! Aunty Seminole—*you* Seminole!'

" 'Why, Tiger-tail?'

" 'Seminole hunt Three-eye long time—hundred, hundred year—hunt 'um Three-eye, kill 'um Three-eye.'

" 'You say that for hundreds of years the Seminoles have hunted a creature with three eyes?'

" 'Sure! Hunt 'um now!'

" '*Now?*'

" 'Sure!'

" 'But, Tiger-tail, if the legends of your people tell you that the Seminoles hunted a creature with three eyes hundreds of years ago, certainly no such three-eyed creatures remain today?'

" 'Some.'

" 'What! Where?'

" 'Black Bayou.'

" 'Do you mean to tell me that a living creature with three eyes still inhabits the forests of Black Bayou?'

" 'Sure. Me see 'um. Me kill 'um three-eye man.'

" 'You have killed a man who had *three eyes?*'

" 'Sure!'

" 'A man? *With three eyes?*'

" 'Sure.' "

The pretty waitress, excitedly engrossed in her story, was unconsciously acting out the thrilling scene of her dialogue with the Indian, even imitating his voice and gestures. And Kemper and I listened and watched her breathlessly, fascinated by her lithe and supple grace as well as by the astounding story she was so frankly unfolding with the consummate artlessness of a natural actress.

She turned her flushed face to us:

"I made up my mind," she said, "that Tiger-tail's story was worth investigating. It was perfectly easy for me to secure corroboration, because that Seminole went back to his Everglade camp and told every one of his people that I was a white Seminole because my ancestors also hunted the three-eyed man and nobody except a Seminole could know that such a thing as a three-eyed man existed.

"So, the next afternoon off, I embarked in Tiger-tail's canoe and he took me to his camp. And

23

there I talked to his people, men and women, questioning, listening, putting this and that together, trying to discover some foundation for their persistent statements concerning men, still living in the jungles of Black Bayou, who had three eyes instead of two.

"All told the same story; all asserted that since the time their records ran the Seminoles had hunted and slain every three-eyed man they could catch; and that as long as the Seminoles had lived in the Everglades the three-eyed men had lived in the forests beyond Black Bayou."

She paused, dramatically, cooling her cheeks in her palms and looking from Kemper to me with eyes made starry by excitement.

"And *what* do you think!" she continued, under her breath. "To prove what they said they brought for my inspection a skull. And then two more skulls like the first one.

"Every skull had been painted with Spanish red; the coarse black hair still stuck to the scalps. And, behind, just over where the pituitary gland is situated, was a hollow, bony orbit—unmistakably the socket of a *third eye!*"

24

"W-where are those skulls?" demanded Kemper, in a voice not entirely under control.

"They wouldn'ι part with one of them. I tried every possible persuasion. On my own responsibility, and even before I communicated with Mr. Smith—" turning toward me, "—I offered them twenty thousand dollars for a single skull, staking my word of honour that the Bronx Museum would pay that sum.

"It was useless. Not only do the Seminoles refuse to part with one of those skulls, but I have also learned that I am the first person with a white skin who has ever even heard of their existence—so profoundly have these red men of the Everglades guarded their secret through centuries."

After a silence Kemper, rather pale, remarked:

"This is a most astonishing business, Miss Grey."

"What do you think about it?" I demanded. "Is it not worth while for us to explore Black Bayou?"

He nodded in a dazed sort of way, but his gaze remained riveted on the girl. Presently he said:

"Why does Miss Grey go?"

She turned in surprise:

"Why am I going? But it is *my* discovery—*my* contribution to science, isn't it?"

"Certainly!" we exclaimed warmly and in unison. And Kemper added: "I was only thinking of the dangers and hardships. Smith and I could do the actual work——"

"Oh!" she cried in quick protest, "I wouldn't miss one moment of the excitement, one pain, one pang! I *love* it! It would simply break my heart not to share every chance, hazard, danger of this expedition—every atom of hope, excitement, despair, uncertainty—and the ultimate success—the unsurpassable thrill of exultation in the final instant of triumph!"

She sprang to her feet in a flash of uncontrollable enthusiasm, and stood there, aglow with courage and resolution, making a highly agreeable picture in her apron and cuffs, the sea wind fluttering the bright tendrils of her hair under her dainty cap.

We got to our feet much impressed; and now absolutely convinced that there did exist, somewhere, descendants of prehistoric men in whom the third eye—placed in the back of the head for purposes of defensive observation—had not become obsolete and reduced to the traces which we know only as the pituitary body or pituitary gland.

Kemper and I were, of course, aware that in the insect world the ocelli served the same purpose that the degenerate pituitary body once served in the occiput of man.

As we three walked slowly back to the campfire, where our evening meal was now ready, Evelyn Grey, who walked between us, told us what she knew about the hunting of these three-eyed men by the Seminoles—how intense was the hatred of the Indians for these people, how murderously they behaved toward any one of them whom they could track down and catch.

"Tiger-tail told me," she went on, "that in all probability the strange race was nearing extinction, but that all had not yet been exterminated because now and then, when hunting along Black Bayou, traces of living three-eyed men were still found by him and his people.

"No later than last week Tiger-tail himself had startled one of these strange denizens of Black Bayou from a meal of fish; and had heard him leap through the bushes and plunge into the water.

It appears that centuries of persecution have made these three-eyed men partly amphibious—that is, capable of filling their lungs with air and remaining under water almost as long as a turtle."

"That's impossible!" said Kemper bluntly.

"I thought so myself," she said with a smile, "until Tiger-tail told me a little more about them. He says that they can breathe through the pores of their skins; that their bodies are covered with a thick, silky hair, and that when they dive they carry down with them enough air to form a sort of skin over them, so that under water their bodies appear to be silver-plated."

"Good Lord!" faltered Kemper. "That is a little too much!"

"Yet," said I, "that is exactly what air-breathing water beetles do. The globules of air, clinging to the body-hairs, appear to silver-plate them; and they can remain below indefinitely, breathing through spiracles. Doubtless the skin pores of these men have taken on the character of spiracles."

"You know," he said in a curious, flat voice, which sounded like the tones of a partly stupified man, "this whole business is so grotesque—apparently so wildly absurd—that it's having a sort of nightmare effect on me." And, dropping his voice to a whisper close to my ear: "Good heavens!" he said. "Can you reconcile such a creature as we are starting out to hunt, with anything living known to science?"

"No," I replied in guarded tones. "And there are moments, Kemper, since I have come into possession of Miss Grey's story, when I find myself seriously doubting my own sanity."

"I'm doubting mine, now," he whispered, "only that girl is so fresh and wholesome and human and sane——"

"She is a very clever girl," I said.

"And really beautiful!"

"She is intelligent," I remarked. There was a chill in my tone which doubtless discouraged Kemper, for he ventured nothing further concerning her superficially personal attractions.

After all, if any questions of priority were to arise, the pretty waitress was *my* discovery. And in the scientific world it is an inflexible rule that he who first discovers any particular specimen of any species whatever is first entitled to describe and comment upon that specimen without interference or unsolicited advice from anybody.

Maybe there was in my eye something that expressed as much. For when Kemper caught my cold gaze fixed upon him he winced and looked away like a reproved setter dog who knew better. Which also, for the moment, put an end to the rather gay and frivolous line of small talk which he had again begun with the pretty waitress.

I was exceedingly surprised at Professor William Henry Kemper, D.F.

As we approached the campfire the loathsome odour of frying mullet saluted my nostrils.

Kemper, glancing at Grue, said aside to me:

"That's an odd-looking fellow. What is he? Minorcan?"

"Oh, just a beachcomber. I don't know what he is. He strikes me as dirty—though he can't be so, physically. I don't like him and I don't know why. And I wish we'd engaged somebody else to guide us."

Toward dawn something awoke me and I sat up

in my blanket under the moon. But my leg had not been pulled.

Kemper snored at my side. In her little dog-tent the pretty waitress probably was fast asleep. I knew it because the string she had tied to one of her ornamental ankles still lay across the ground convenient to my hand. In any emergency I had only to pull it to awake her.

A similar string, tied to my ankle, ran parallel to hers and disappeared under the flap of her tent. This was for her to pull if she liked. She had never yet pulled it. Nor I the other. Nevertheless I truly felt that these humble strings were, in a subtler sense, ties that bound us together. No wonder Kemper's behaviour had slightly irritated me.

I looked up at the silver moon; I glanced at Kemper's unlovely bulk, swathed in a blanket; I contemplated the dog-tent with, perhaps, that slight trace of sentiment which a semi-tropical moon is likely to inspire even in a jellyfish. And suddenly I remembered Grue and looked for him.

He was accustomed to sleep in his boat, but I did not see him in either of the boats. Here and there were a few lumpy shadows in the moonlight, but none of them was Grue lying prone on the ground. Where the devil had he gone?

Cautiously I untied my ankle string, rose in my pajamas, stepped into my slippers, and walked out through the moonlight.

There was nothing to hide Grue, no rocks or vegetation except the solitary palm on the backbone of the reef.

I walked as far as the tree and looked up into the arching fronds. Nobody was up there. I could see the moonlit sky through the fronds. Nor was Grue lying asleep anywhere on the other side of the coral ridge.

And suddenly I became aware of all my latent distrust and dislike for the man. And the vigour of my sentiments surprised me because I really had not understood how deep and thorough my dislike had been.

Also, his utter disappearance struck me as uncanny. Both boats were there; and there were many leagues of sea to the nearest coast.

Troubled and puzzled I turned and walked back to the dead embers of the fire. Kemper had merely changed the timbre of his snore to a whistling aria, which at any other time would have enraged me. Now, somehow, it almost comforted me.

Seated on the shore I looked out to sea, racking my brains for an explanation of Grue's disappearance. And while I sat there racking them, far out on the water a little flock of ducks suddenly scattered and rose with frightened quackings and furiously beating wings.

For a moment I thought I saw a round, dark object on the waves where the flock had been.

And while I sat there watching, up out of the sea along the reef to my right crawled a naked, dripping figure holding a dead duck in his mouth.

Fascinated, I watched it, recognising Grue with his ratty black hair all plastered over his face.

Whether he caught sight of me or not, I don't know; but he suddenly dropped the dead duck from his mouth, turned, and dived under water.

It was a grim and horrid species of sport or pastime, this amphibious business of his, catching wild birds and dragging them about as though he were an animal.

Evidently he was ashamed of himself, for he had dropped the duck. I watched it floating by on the waves, its head under water. Suddenly something jerked it under, a fish perhaps, for it did not come up and float again, as far as I could see.

When I went back to camp Grue lay apparently asleep on the north side of the fire. I glanced at him in disgust and crawled into my tent.

The next day Evelyn Grey awoke with a headache and kept her tent. I had all I could do to prevent Kemper from prescribing for her. I did that myself, sitting beside her and testing her pulse for hours at a time, while Kemper took one of Grue's grains and went off into the mangroves and speared grunt and eels for a chowder which he said he knew how to concoct.

Toward afternoon the pretty waitress felt much better, and I warned Kemper and Grue that we should sail for Black Bayou after dinner.

Dinner was a mess, as usual, consisting of fried mullet and rice, and a sort of chowder in which the only ingredients I recognised were sections of crayfish.

After we had finished and had withdrawn from the fire, Grue scraped every remaining shred of

"To see him feed made me sick."

food into a kettle and went for it. To see him feed made me sick, so I rejoined Miss Grey and Kemper, who had found a green cocoanut and were alternately deriving nourishment from the milk inside it.

Somehow or other there seemed to me a certain levity about that performance, and it made me uncomfortable; but I managed to smile a rather sickly smile when they offered me a draught, and I took a pull at the milk—I don't exactly know why, because I don't like it. But the moon was up over the sea, now, and the dusk was languorously balmy, and I didn't care to leave those two drinking milk out of the same cocoanut under a tropic moon.

Not that my interest in Evelyn Grey was other than scientific. But after all it was I who had discovered her.

We sailed as soon as Grue, gobbling and snuffling, had cleaned up the last crumb of food. Kemper blandly offered to take Miss Grey into his boat, saying that he feared my boat was overcrowded, what with the paraphernalia, the folding cages, Grue, Miss Grey, and myself.

36

I sat on that suggestion, but offered to take my own tiller and lend him Grue. He couldn't wriggle out of it, seeing that his alleged motive had been the overcrowding of my boat, but he looked rather sick when Grue went aboard his boat.

As for me, I hoisted sail with something so near a chuckle that it surprised me; and I looked at Evelyn Grey to see whether she had noticed the unseemly symptom.

Apparently she had not. She sat forward, her eyes fixed soulfully upon the moon. Had I been dedicated to any profession except a scientific one —but let that pass.

Grue in Kemper's sail-boat led, and my boat followed out into the silvery and purple dusk, now all sparkling under the high lustre of the moon.

Dimly I saw vast rafts of wild duck part and swim leisurely away to port and starboard, leaving a glittering lane of water for us to sail through; into the scintillant night from the sea sprang mullet, silvery, quivering, falling back into the wash with a splash.

Here and there in the moonlight steered ominous

37

black triangles, circling us, leading us, sheering across bow and flashing wake, all phosphorescent with lambent sea-fire—the fins of great sharks.

"You need have no fear," said I to the pretty waitress.

She said nothing.

"Of course if you *are* afraid," I added, "perhaps you might care to change your seat."

There was room in the stern where I sat.

"Do you think there is any danger?" she asked.

"From sharks?"

"Yes."

"Reaching up and biting you?"

"Yes."

"Oh, I don't really suppose there is," I said, managing to convey the idea, I am ashamed to say, that the catastrophe was a possibility.

She came over and seated herself beside me. I was very much ashamed of myself, but I could not repress a triumphant glance ahead at the other boat, where Kemper sat huddled forward, evidently bored to extinction.

Every now and then I could see him turn and

crane his neck as though in an effort to distinguish what was going on in our boat.

There was nothing going on, absolutely nothing. The moon was magnificent; and I think the pretty waitress must have been a little tired, for her head drooped and nodded at moments, even while I was talking to her about a specimen of *Euplectilla speciosa* on which I had written a monograph. So she must have been really tired, for the subject was interesting.

"You won't incommode my operations with sheet and tiller," I said to her kindly, "if you care to rest your head against my shoulder."

Evidently she was very tired, for she did so, and closed her eyes.

After a while, fearing that she might fall over backward into the sea—but let that pass. . . . I don't know whether or not Kemper could distinguish anything aboard our boat. He craned his head enough to twist it off his neck.

To be so utterly, so blindly devoted to science is a great safeguard for a man. Single-mindedness, however, need not induce atrophy of every humane impulse. I drew the pretty waitress closer

39

—not that the night was cold, but it might become so. Changes in the tropics come swiftly. It is well to be prepared.

Her cheek felt very soft against my shoulder. There seemed to be a faint perfume about her hair. It really was odd how subtly fragrant she seemed to be—almost, perhaps, a matter of scientific interest.

Her hands did not seem to be chilled; they did seem unusually smooth and soft.

I said to her: "When at home, I suppose your mother tucks you in; doesn't she?"

"Yes," she nodded sleepily.

"And what does she do then?" said I, with something of that ponderous playfulness with which I make scientific jokes at a meeting of the Bronx Anthropological Association, when I preside.

"She kisses me and turns out the light," said Evelyn Grey, innocently.

I don't know how much Kemper could distinguish. He kept dodging about and twisting his head until I really thought it would come off, unless it had been screwed on like the top of a piano stool.

A few minutes later he fired his pistol twice; and Evelyn sat up. I never knew why he fired; he never offered any explanation.

Toward midnight I could hear the roar of breakers on our starboard bow. Evelyn heard them, too, and sat up inquiringly.

"Grue has found the inlet to Black Bayou, I suppose," said I.

And it proved to be the case, for, with the surf thundering on either hand, we sailed into a smoothly flowing inlet through which the flood tide was running between high dunes all sparkling in the moonlight and crowned with shadowy palms.

Occasionally I heard noises ahead of us from the other boat, as though Kemper was trying to converse with us, but as his apropos was as unintelligible as it was inopportune, I pretended not to hear him. Besides, I had all I could do to manoeuvre the tiller and prevent Evelyn Grey from falling off backward into the bayou. Besides, it is not customary to converse with the man at the helm.

After a while—during which I seemed to distinguish in Kemper's voice a quality that rhymes

with his name—his tones varied through phases all
the way from irony to exasperation. After a while
he gave it up and took to singing.

There was a moon, and I suppose he thought he
had a voice. It didn't strike me so. After several
somewhat melancholy songs, he let off his pistol
two or three times and then subsided into silence.

I didn't care; neither his songs nor his shots interrupted—but let that pass, also.

We were now sailing into the forest through
pool after pool of interminable lagoons, startling
into unseen and clattering flight hundreds of water-
fowl. I could feel the wind from their whistling
wings in the darkness, as they drove by us out to
sea. It seemed to startle the pretty waitress. It
is a solemn thing to be responsible for a pretty
girl's peace of mind. I reassured her continually,
perhaps a trifle nervously. But there were no more
pistol shots. Perhaps Kemper had used up his
cartridges.

We were still drifting along under drooping sails,
borne inland almost entirely by the tide, when the
first pale, watery, gray light streaked the east.
When it grew a little lighter, Evelyn sat up, all

danger of sharks being over. Also, I could begin to see what was going on in the other boat. Which was nothing remarkable; Kemper slumped against the mast, his head turned in our direction; Grue sat at the helm, motionless, his tattered straw hat sagging on his neck.

When the sun rose, I called out cheerily to Kemper, asking him how he had passed the night. Evelyn also raised her head, pausing while bringing her disordered hair under discipline, to listen to his reply.

But he merely mumbled something. Perhaps he was still sleepy.

As for me, I felt exceedingly well; and when Grue turned his craft in shore, I did so, too; and when, under the overhanging foliage of the forest, the nose of my boat grated on the sand, I rose and crossed the deck with a step distinctly frolicsome.

Kemper seemed distant and glum; Evelyn Grey spoke to him shyly now and then, and I noticed she looked at him only when he was gazing elsewhere than at her. She had a funny, conciliatory air with him, half ashamed, partly humorous and amused, as though something about Kemper's sulky ill-humour was continually making tiny in-roads on her gravity.

Some mullet had jumped into the two boats—half a dozen during our moonlight voyage—and these were now being fried with rice for us by Grue. Lord! How I hated to eat them!

After we had finished breakfast, Grue, as usual, did everything to the remainder except to get into the fry-pan with both feet; and as usual he sickened me.

When he'd cleaned up everything, I sent him off into the forest to find a dry shell-mound for camping purposes; then I made fast both boats, and Kemper and I carried ashore our paraphernalia, spare *batterie-de-cuisine*, firearms, fishing tackle, spears, harpoons, grains, oars, sails, spars, folding cage—everything with which a strictly scientific expedition is usually burdened.

Evelyn was washing her face in the crystal waters of a branch that flowed into the lagoon from under the live-oaks. She looked very pretty doing it, like a naiad or dryad scrubbing away at her forest toilet.

It was, in fact, such a pretty spectacle that I was

going over to sit beside her while she did it, but Kemper started just when I was going to, and I turned away. Some men invariably do the wrong thing. But a handsome man doesn't last long with a pretty girl.

I was thinking of this as I stood contemplating an alligator slide, when Grue came back saying that the shore on which we had landed was the termination of a shell-mound, and that it was the only dry place be had found.

So I bade him pitch our tents a few feet back from the shore; and stood watching him while he did so, one eye reverting occasionally to Evelyn Grey and Kemper. They both were seated cross-legged beside the branch, and they seemed to be talking a great deal and rather earnestly. I couldn't quite understand what they found to talk about so earnestly and volubly all of a sudden, inasmuch as they had heretofore exchanged very few observations during a most brief and formal acquaintance, dating only from sundown the day before.

Grue set up our three tents, carried the luggage inland, and then hung about for a while until the vast shadow of a vulture swept across the trees.

I never saw such an indescribable expression on a human face as I saw on Grue's as he looked up at the huge, unclean bird. His vitreous eyes fairly glittered; the corners of his mouth quivered and grew wet; and to my astonishment he seemed to emit a low, mewing noise.

"What the devil are you doing?" I said impulsively, in my amazement and disgust.

He looked at me, his eyes still glittering, the corners of his mouth still wet; but the curious sounds had ceased.

"What?" he asked.

"Nothing. I thought you spoke." I didn't know what else to say.

He made no reply. Once, when I had partly turned my head, I was aware that he was warily turning his to look at the vulture, which had alighted heavily on the ground near the entrails and heads of the mullet, where he had cast them on the dead leaves.

I walked over to where Evelyn Grey and Kemper sat so busily conversing; and their volubility ceased as they glanced up and saw me approaching. Which phenomenon both perplexed and displeased me.

I said:

"This is the Black Bayou forest, and we have the most serious business of our lives before us. Suppose you and I start out, Kemper, and see if there are any traces of what we are after in the neighborhood of our camp."

"Do you think it safe to leave Miss Grey alone in camp?" he asked gravely.

I hadn't thought of that:

"No, of course not," I said. "Grue can stay."

"I don't need anybody," she said quickly. "Anyway, I'm rather afraid of Grue."

"Afraid of Grue?" I repeated.

"Not exactly afraid. But he's—unpleasant."

"I'll remain with Miss Grey," said Kemper politely.

"Oh," she exclaimed, "I couldn't ask that. It is true that I feel a little tired and nervous, but I can go with you and Mr. Smith and Grue——"

I surveyed Kemper in cold perplexity. As chief of the expedition, I couldn't very well offer to re-

47

main with Evelyn Grey, but I didn't propose that Kemper should, either.

"Take Grue," he suggested, "and look about the woods for a while. Perhaps after dinner Miss Grey may feel sufficiently rested to join us."

"I am sure," she said, "that a few hours' rest in camp will set me on my feet. All I need is rest. I didn't sleep very soundly last night."

I felt myself growing red, and I looked away from them both.

"Oh," said Kemper, in apparent surprise, "I thought you had slept soundly all night long."

"Nobody," said I, "could have slept very pleasantly during that musical performance of yours."

"Were you singing?" she asked innocently of Kemper.

"He was singing when he wasn't firing off his pistol," I remarked. "No wonder you couldn't sleep with any satisfaction to yourself."

Grue had disappeared into the forest; I stood watching for him to come out again. After a few minutes I heard a furious but distant noise of flapping; the others also heard it; and we listened in silence, wondering what it was.

"It's Grue killing something," faltered Evelyn Grey, turning a trifle pale.

"Confound it!" I exclaimed. "I'm going to stop that right now."

Kemper rose and followed me as I started for the woods; but as we passed the beached boats Grue appeared from among the trees.

"Where have you been?" I demanded.

"In the woods."

"Doing what?"

"Nothing."

There was a bit of down here and there clinging to his cotton shirt and trousers, and one had caught and stuck at the corner of his mouth.

"See here, Grue," I said, "I don't want you to kill any birds except for camp purposes. Why do you try to catch and kill birds?"

"I don't."

I stared at the man and he stared back at me out of his glassy eyes.

"You mean to say that you don't, somehow or other, manage to catch and kill birds?"

"No, I don't."

There was nothing further for me to say unless

49

I gave him the lie. I didn't care to do that, need-
ing his services.

Evelyn Grey had come up to join us; there was
a brief silence; we all stood looking at Grue; and
he looked back at us out of his pale, washed-out,
and unblinking eyes.

"Grue," I said, "I haven't yet explained to you
the object of this expedition to Black Bayou.
Now, I'll tell you what I want. But first let me
ask you a question or two. You know the Black
Bayou forests, don't you?"

"Yes."

"Did you ever see anything unusual in these
forests?"

"No."

"Are you sure?"

The man stared at us, one after another. Then
he said:

"What are you looking for in Black Bayou?"

"Something very curious, very strange, very unusual. So strange and unusual, in fact, that the
great Zoölogical Society of the Bronx in New York
has sent me down here at the head of this expedition to search the forests of Black Bayou."

50

"For what?" he demanded, in a dull, accentless voice.

"For a totally new species of human being, Grue. I wish to catch one and take it back to New York in that folding cage."

His green eyes had grown narrow as though sun-dazzled. Kemper had stepped behind us into the woods and was now busy setting up the folding cage. Grue remained motionless.

"I am going to offer you," I said, "the sum of one thousand dollars in gold if you can guide us to a spot where we may see this hitherto unknown species—a creature which is apparently a man but which has, in the back of his head, *a third eye*——"

I paused in amazement: Grue's cheeks had suddenly puffed out and were quivering; and from the corners of his slitted mouth he was emitting a whimpering sound like the noise made by a low-circling pigeon.

"Grue!" I cried. "What's the matter with you?"

"What is *he* doing?" screamed Grue, quivering from head to foot, but not turning around.

"Who?" I cried.

"The man behind me!"

51

"Professor Kemper? He's setting up the folding cage———"

With a screech that raised my hair, Grue whipped out his murderous knife and *hurled himself backward* at Kemper, but the latter shrank aside behind the partly erected cage, and Grue whirled around, snarling, hacking, and even biting at the wood frame and steel bars.

And then occurred a thing so horrid that it sickened me to the pit of my stomach; for the man's sagging straw hat had fallen off, and there, in the back of his head, through the coarse, black, ratty hair, I saw a glassy eye glaring at me.

"Kemper!" I shouted. "He's got a third eye! He's one of them! Knock him flat with your riflestock!" And I seized a shot-gun from the top of the baggage bundle on the ground beside me, and leaped at Grue, aiming a terrific blow at him.

But the glassy eye in the back of his head was watching me between the clotted strands of hair, and he dodged both Kemper and me, swinging his heavy knife in circles and glaring at us both out of the front and back of his head.

52

"'Kemper!' I shouted . . . 'He is one of them! Knock him flat with your riflestock!'"

Kemper seized him by his arm, but Grue's shirt came off, and I saw his entire body was as furry as an ape's. And all the while he was snapping at us and leaping hither and thither to avoid our blows; and from the corners of his puffed cheeks he whined and whimpered and mewed through the saliva foam.

"Keep him from the water!" I panted, following him with clubbed shot-gun; and as I advanced I almost stepped on a soiled heap of foulness—the dead buzzard which he had caught and worried to death with his teeth.

Suddenly he threw his knife at my head, hurling it backward; dodged, screeched, and bounded by me toward the shore of the lagoon, where the pretty waitress was standing, petrified.

For one moment I thought he had her, but she picked up her skirts, ran for the nearest boat, and seized a harpoon; and in his fierce eagerness to catch her he leaped clear over the boat and fell with a splash into the lagoon.

As Kemper and I sprang aboard and looked over into the water, we could see him going down out of reach of a harpoon; and his body seemed to be silver-plated, flashing and glittering like a burnished eel, so completely did the skin of air envelope him, held there by the fur that covered him.

And, as he rested for a moment on the bottom, deep down through the clear waters of the lagoon where he lay prone, I could see, as the current stirred his long, black hair, the third eye looking up at us, glassy, unwinking, horrible.

A bubble or two, like globules of quicksilver, were detached from the burnished skin of air that clothed him, and came glittering upward.

Suddenly there was a flash; a flurrying cloud of blue mud; and Grue was gone.

After a long while I turned around in the muteness of my despair. And slowly froze.

For the pretty waitress, becomingly pale, was gathered in Kemper's arms, her cheek against his shoulder. Neither seemed to be aware of me.

"Darling," he said, in the imbecile voice of a man in love, "why do you tremble so when I am here to protect you? Don't you love and trust me?"

"Oo—h—yes," she sighed, pressing her cheek closer to his shoulder.

I shoved my hands into my pockets, passed them without noticing them, and stepped ashore.

And there I sat down under a tree, with my back toward them, all alone and face to face with the greatest grief of my life.

But which it was—the loss of her or the loss of Grue, I had not yet made up my mind.

THE SPACE ANNIHILATOR.[1]

N the afternoon of Saturday, August 18, 1900, as I was looking over the daily paper after my return from the Blendheim Electric Works, where I am employed, I noticed in the advertising department the following :

IMPORTANT NOTICE TO ENGINEERS AND SCIENTIFIC MEN.

Ten thousand dollars will be paid to the man or woman duplicating an instrument now in the possession of this company ——

That was as far as I read. Some cheap advertising scheme, I thought, and immediately forgot all about the paragraph.

When, however, towards the last of the month, I received the regular issue of my pet scientific paper, I saw on the first page the same glaring announcement. The fact of the notice being in that paper was guarantee that the offer was bona fide, and I looked the article over carefully.

In addition to the foregoing, the advertisement went on to state that one of a pair of seisma-phones, an invention with patent pending and not yet in the market, had been lost. The in-ventor was dead, and no one had as yet been able to construct an instrument similar to the one now in the company's possession.

Further particulars would be sent to any one satisfying the company that his request for the same was not prompted by idle curiosity, but by a desire to aid science in replacing the lost instrument.

Then came the greatest surprise of all; for, signed at the bottom of this interesting state-ment, as the man representing the company, was the name of Randolph R. Churchill, Patent Office, Washington, D. C.

Now Ranny Churchill and I had been room-mates at college, and I had had many a pleasant visit in his comfortable home on Fourteenth Street. He had graduated from a technical school, taken a course in patent law, and soon after secured a position as one of the govern-mental inspectors of patents in Washington.

My annual vacation was to begin the next week, so I planned a brief trip to Washington to see the wonderful invention which no one had apparently been able to duplicate. I did not write to Churchill, but dropped in on him un-expectedly Saturday night, September 1.

I had seen him two years before down on the

Cape ; and I could scarcely believe that the tired, careworn man who greeted me on my arrival at the Fourteenth Street house was the same merry, light-hearted Randolph Churchill I had hunted and fished with only a couple of summers ago.

He seemed like a man living in constant expectation of something terrible about to happen, and, even before our first greetings were over, I noticed that he paused two or three times and listened intently.

" I think I can guess to what I owe this visit," he said as he went up-stairs with me to my room, "and I would to God I thought you would be able to accomplish what has so far proved impossible."

I told him that it was owing to his advertisement that my present trip had been undertaken, and begged him to tell me more about the wonderful invention.

" Wait till after dinner," he said, "for it is a long story. We will go to my room, and I will tell you then a tale as strange as it is true."

That dinner was the most dismal affair I ever attended. Churchill sat like a man in a trance, completely absorbed in his meditations ; and twice, after listening as I had seen him on my first arrival, he excused himself and left the table abruptly.

" You and Rannie are such old friends, you mustn't mind him to-night," Mrs. Churchill said to me apologetically, while he was out of the

room ; "this terrible affair of the seismaphone
has upset us both completely."

That was the only mention of the subject
during dinner ; but after we had sat in the library
a little while discussing trivial topics, such as
Robert's progress in school and the new furnish-
ings of the house since my last visit, Churchill
and I excused ourselves and went to his private
room.

"I may as well start at the very beginning,"
he said as he threw himself down languidly in
an easy chair, after drawing out from under the
table a long, narrow box, which he placed in his
lap.

"On the night of the tenth of last June the
maid brought me the card of a man who was
waiting down-stairs, and who said he wanted to
see me on very important private business. I
glanced at the name scrawled in red ink on the
bit of card-board, 'Martin M. Bradley,' and wondered vaguely who the man could be, as I did
not remember ever having heard of him before.

"I told the maid to show him up here to the
den, and a few minutes later she ushered into
this room the man who has been the cause of
these gray hairs.

"He was short and sallow, about thirty-five
years of age, as I afterwards found out, though
care and privations had marked him so harshly
that he looked to be nearly fifty. He carried in
his hand this black, leather-covered box which

you see in my lap; and, after seating himself at my invitation, began:

"'You are no doubt surprised, Mr. Churchill, to have a visit from me, for you probably don't remember ever having heard of me before; but I've come to you because I know you are in the patent office, and used to be a friend of mine back in the seventies, and because, too, I've got something so valuable here that I don't dare to send it up to the office in the usual way.'

"He unstrapped, as he spoke, the box, which he had not let out of his hands since he entered, and took from it two black, galvanized rubber instruments, one of which you see here."

Churchill lifted from the case a thing which resembled more than anything else the receiver of a telephone, except that both ends were turned out like the one you put to the ear. He unscrewed this outer cap and handed both parts to me to examine.

About two inches in from the bell-shaped end of the cylinder was a diaphragm of peculiar looking metal, which from appearance I judged to be an alloy of copper and zinc, with something else included. Immediately over this, and tightly stretched across at unequal distances apart, were some twenty fine German silver wires.

"Bradley opened one of the instruments, as I have just done," continued Churchill, "and proceeded to explain to me its construction.

"'These two instruments,' said he, 'which

55

together I call the Martin Bradley Seismaphone, are to the telephone what telegraphy without wires is to the ordinary method of sending messages. Both light and sound, as you know, travel by waves which produce sensation ; one by striking against the retina of the eye, the other by striking on the drum of the ear.

" 'The light wave travels with a velocity of something over 185,000 miles a second, while the sound wave moves much slower. This difference, however, is overcome by the mechanical device in the tube-like section in the middle part of the instrument.

" 'As you have seen the sun's rays collected and focused to one small spot by a reading glass, and the power intensified so that combustion takes place, so in a similar way does the seismaphone collect the sound waves, intensify and bring them to a focus here,' and he indicated with his finger a point back of the metal diaphragm.

" 'By speaking into one of these instruments the sound passes through the wires, and strikes against the metal disk. This sets in motion a series of waves, which, traveling with the enormous velocity of which I have spoken, produce such rapid vibrations that the ear, unaided, cannot perceive the sound, but by means of the other half of the seismaphone these sound waves are collected and so transformed by the corresponding wires and dia-

56

phragm that the voice is reproduced by one instrument in exactly the tone spoken.

" ' By means of the seismaphones, you and I, though separated by thousands of miles, can converse as easily as though we were in the same city, connected by an ordinary metallic current.'

"In a fifteen years' experience with patent seekers, I have met many inventive freaks, and probably something of what I was thinking of his seismaphone showed in my face, for he stopped describing it abruptly, and handing me one of the instruments, said, —

" ' I see you don't believe a word I've told you, and you probably think I'm crazy; so, before I tell you anything more about the construction or possibilities of my invention, I want to ask you to take this half of the seismaphone, and go up to the top of your house. When you are ready to make the test, put the end marked " voice " to your mouth, and say in a distinct tone, " Ready, Bradley." Then, when you see this little hammer striking against the bell, and hear a sharp tinkling inside the cylinder, put the other end to your ear and listen. Oh, you may lock me in as you go out, if you are afraid I may remove any of the bric-à-brac,' he added, as I seemed to hesitate.

" I don't know why it was, for I am not over credulous, but something told me the man was speaking the truth. And when you stop to think of it, what was there so very improbable about it?

"Who would have believed one hundred years ago that we would ever be able to communicate instantaneously with the inhabitants of another continent by any means whatever? Or, to come nearer to our own time, twenty years ago we would have scoffed at the idea of telegraphing without wires. Why, then, was it so impossible to transmit the tones of the human voice without them? It would be only another step in the march of progress.

"I took the instrument and climbed to the garret without a word. Placing the end he had indicated to my lips, I said loudly, 'Ready, Bradley.' Without any special expectation I then put the other end to my ear, and at the result nearly fell over backwards; for, as distinctly as if the man I had left down-stairs had been standing beside me, I heard him say, —

"'Don't speak so loud. I can hear you at this distance if you merely whisper. Now press the little button at the end marked "ear," and wait for the megaphone attachment.' I did as he said, and again I jumped and nearly dropped the instrument, for the room was filled with a voice which sounded louder than a peal of thunder.

"'By pressing that button you do for the seismaphone what by putting on the horns you do for the phonograph or graphophone,' the stentorian voice said. 'You had better press the button in the other end, for my voice with this attachment is probably too loud for pleasure.'

"I pressed the button obediently as directed, and walked back down-stairs filled with wonder.

"We shall not get to bed any earlier than Martin Bradley and I did that night, if I stop to tell you all of our conversation. I found that he was a man I had known slightly some years ago when I was trying for the patent office position.

"He had in his youth been through a technical school and received a good education; but had been unable to settle down to any steady employment, preferring to devote himself to some great invention. Eight years ago he began working on this instrument, and had been developing and perfecting it ever since.

"The proposition he made me was that I should go into partnership with him to get the seismaphone patented and before the public, he furnishing the device, and I the money and backing.

"We sat and talked for hours, and the morning sun found us still in our chairs discussing the immense possibilities of the invention.

"It would supersede the mails. Speaking-tubes, telephones, telegraphs, and cables would give way to it. In short, the inventor of such an instrument would win for himself a name greater than a Morse or an Edison, and the fortune he could amass would exceed that of all the Vanderbilts, Goulds, and Rockefellers in the country.

"Martin Bradley remained at my house all that week, and had the best of everything that money could buy. I secured a two weeks' vacation from the patent office, and he and I worked together every hour of that time.

"One day as a test he took one-half of the seismaphone and went down the Potomac a hundred and forty miles to Point Lookout, while I stayed at home with the other instrument. He had by use of the long-distance telephone hired a man down there to keep watch for the arrival of the boat he was coming on, and given him instructions to telephone me when it first hove in sight.

"I sent Nellie and the children out to Chevy Chase for the day, and sat all the afternoon in front of the telephone, with the seismaphone on my knee. Several times I called to Bradley, but he did not answer.

"About three o'clock, however, the 'phone rang; and, just as I had got connection, and began talking with the man down at the Point, I saw the little hammer of the seismaphone vibrating, and, putting the instrument to my ear, heard Martin Bradley say distinctly : ' Have just sighted the lighthouse, so get down to the telephone for a message.'

"I turned to the telephone, and, sure enough, the man at the other end of the wire was telling me that the Petrel was in sight. As the boat neared the shore, Bradley kept up a running comment on events that took place.

"'We're just pulling up the flag and firing a salute,' he called; and scarcely did I catch his words when from the telephone at my ear, as if in echo, came the message, 'They have just run up a flag and are firing a salute.'

"During the next week we tried every kind of test imaginable with the seismaphone, and there was not a flaw in its workings.

"I was perfectly satisfied, and had started proceedings to secure a patent, when the first news of the recent trouble in China came; and then, for two weeks, as you know, the various legations were regularly slaughtered one day and reported safe on the following.

"Martin Bradley was so excited that he nearly forgot his seismaphone. In the course of his wanderings he had lived for two years in Northern China, and could talk the lingo like a native, and was wild to go out there as a newspaper correspondent.

"One day he came rushing to my room with a copy of a morning paper in his hand.

"'See that,' he cried excitedly, 'this paper says that Minister Conger was butchered in cold blood June 24, and all the others of the legation tortured to death by those yellow devils. To-morrow if you buy a paper you will read that they are safe and well. I tell you, I am going to China to find out for myself the truth of this matter, and when I do the world shall know what is true and what is false. They can put restrictions on the press, the telegraph, and the cables, but they can't restrict Martin Bradley's seismaphone.

" 'Just think of the advertisement for the invention, too,' he continued, getting more and more excited. 'Every reading person in the world will know that the truth was finally obtained through Martin Bradley, by means of his greatest of all inventions, the seismaphone.'

"I tried to dissuade him, telling him of the terrible risk he would run, but he would not listen. He had lived in Peking for two years, he said, and knew the city perfectly and the customs and language of the people.

" He scraped together three hundred dollars some way, the Lord only knows how, engaged a berth for San Francisco, and inside three days had made all preparations for the trip. When I found that nothing I could say or do made any difference, I gave up arguing and helped him all I could.

" He knew what he wanted, though, so much better than I that the only practical assistance I gave him was of the financial kind. I arranged credit for him at the British bank of Hong Kong and Shanghai, and furnished all the money needed for his traveling expenses.

" He purchased a complete Chinese disguise

from a Washington costumer, and when one
night, before leaving, he appeared before me, a
long black cue hanging down his back, his
face stained, and chattering the disjointed dia-
lect he had learned during his two years' stay
in Peking, I felt a little hope that his scheme,
daring as it was, might succeed.

"I heard from him several times each day,
all along the journey to San Francisco. Every
time he grew tired or lonesome he called me up
and told me of the country he was passing
through, while I kept him informed of what
was going on back here in Washington.

"For a whole week after he left San Francisco I didn't hear a word from him, though I
kept the seismaphone with me all the time, and
I was growing terribly worried, when one night
he signaled and I heard a weak voice saying,
'Oh, Lord, I've been so seasick, I didn't care
for one while whether there was any such place
as China or not, and the thought of the seismaphone never entered my head.'

"After landing at Hong Kong he had to wait
two days before starting for Shanghai, but he
had to be resigned, and I never spent a pleas-
anter afternoon in my life than that day when
I sat in the patent office and heard him describing his trip about Victoria, that beautiful possession of the British crown.

"He put on the megaphone attachment while
he was being wheeled about in a little jinrikisha,

and I could hear him talking to the coolie who pulled it, and the squeaking of the wheels, as plainly as the scratching of the pens over where the clerks sat writing in my office.

"All the men at the office thought me crazy, and I don't know as I blame them, for of course I hadn't taken any of them into my confidence, and it is rather an unusual sight to see a man stop in the midst of a conversation with you, put an unconnected receiver up to his ear, then start talking apparently with the empty air.

"I had to take Nellie into the secret after a while, though, for she, too, thought I must be insane, and smuggled a couple of doctors up to the house to dinner one night to watch me. I told Bradley, and he submitted to the necessary evil, as he called it.

"So, while he was in Shanghai, describing one of the Chinese pagodas to me (at twelve o'clock at night, mind you) I awakened her and let her take the seismaphone, and you never saw a more excited woman. She sat up all the rest of the night, listening to Bradley and asking him questions.

"Towards morning I told her to throw in the megaphone attachment, and the instrument was laid up for four days, for she was so frightened at the loudness of the voice that she dropped the seismaphone, and two of the German silver wires snapped. I was nearly crazy in fact for

64

the next few days, for I thought that the instrument was ruined.

"I couldn't tell whether Bradley was getting my messages all right or not, and not a word did I hear from him during all that time.

"After working all one night, however, I succeeded in getting the wires fixed in the right position and signaled to Bradley. Almost immediately he answered and I heard him shouting :—

"'What the devil has happened to you? Have you been seasick too? I haven't heard a word from you for four days, and here I've been sending you the most exciting kind of messages. The disguise is working fine, and I shall soon be in the city of Peking.'

"That day I received a note from the head of my department, telling me I was granted an indefinite leave of absence, and I haven't been in the office since. They think me a lunatic, and God knows I've been through enough to make a maniac of any man.

"For three days more I didn't get a message from Bradley, and I had begun to fear that the wires I had fixed weren't right, when the bell started to tinkle and I heard him signaling faintly.

"'This is the last time you will ever hear from me,' he said, and I noticed that he spoke as if in great pain. 'I worked my way into the city last night, but got mixed up in a street fight between the imperial troops and a crowd of ruffians and was captured by the latter, who found out my disguise.

"'Don't interrupt me,' he called faintly, for I had uttered an exclamation of horror, and he, seeing the hammer striking, thought I was trying to speak to him, 'for I can't hear if you do. They cut my ears off this morning, and filled up the holes with hot wax.

"'There are three Englishmen and a Russian here also, all of whom were captured and brought in to-day.'

"He stopped for a few minutes, and I stood cursing the helplessness of the whole thing. There he was, thousands of miles away, being tortured to death in some filthy Chinese den, and I had to stand and listen calmly to his voice, not able to raise a hand to aid him.

"'I give you my share in the seismaphone,' he continued after a while, 'and I pray you may be able tó duplicate the half you now have, for you will never see this one again. The two instruments are exactly alike, except for the wiring, and that you will have to get by experiment, for all my data have been destroyed.'

"Then he must have fainted, for he stopped suddenly, and I heard a voice, probably that of one of the Englishmen, saying, 'Poor devil, I wish I could get to him ; but they've tied me to this ring in the wall, and I can't move a foot.'

"I didn't hear another word till late that

night, when I woke up to find Nellie by my bed, pale and trembling.

"'Don't you hear him calling you?' she gasped.

"I seized the seismaphone, pressed the button, and, in the silence of the night, I heard Martin Bradley wailing, 'Churchill — Churchill.'

"I spoke into the thing, so that his bell would ring, and he would know that I was listening.

"'Good-by,' he called. 'They are killing us off one by one. The Russian, and two of the Englishmen are dead now, and it's my turn next. They've just brought in an American, and he told me on his fingers that the lega- tions ——'

"That was as far as he got. I heard a ter- rible screeching, which drowned out his voice ; and suddenly all was quiet.

"Three times since that some of those heathen have got hold of the thing; but that death message of Bradley's is the last English word that has come over the seismaphone.

"The third time I heard them at it, I threw in the megaphone attachment, and shouted as loud as I could. Since then not a sound has come from the instrument.

"I put the advertisement you saw in the papers ; but though hundreds of men have tried, no one has been able to duplicate the part of the seismaphone I now have. Some have re-

fused even to try, when I explained what was
wanted, for they thought me either crazy or
a fool.

"I hoped at first that some one might be able
to replace the loss, but now I know it cannot
be done. Bradley told me that it took him
three years to determine the distances at which
the wires had to be placed, and he alone knew
the principle on which the whole mechanism
depends.

"No one has ever been able to duplicate the
diaphragm. It is a curious alloy of copper,
zinc, and some other metal ; but what that third
metal is, no one can determine."

Churchill had finished his strange story ; and
now he leaned back in his chair, his face gray
and set. Outside the noise of a great city
waking to another day's life could be heard,
and somewhere in the house I heard a clock
slowly strike five.

I picked up the seismaphone from the table
and brought it over to the light. Then, even
as I held it in my hand, I saw the little hammer begin vibrating rapidly, and heard the
tinkling of the bell.

But Randolph Churchill had heard that signal too, and starting from his chair, he snatched
the instrument from my hands, and held it to
his car.

"It's only those damned heathen at it again,"
he groaned, and threw the thing on the table.

68

In falling it must have pressed the tiny button, which threw on the megaphone attachment. The little bell began ringing again, and I started back, trembling with a strange mixture of fear and awe.

For, above the clatter of the wagons, and the grinding of the cars as they climbed Fourteenth Street hill, there, in that little room, fifteen thousand miles from the Celestial Empire, I heard a confused bable of many voices, howling and cursing in the Chinese tongue.

A CORNER IN LIGHTNING

I

THEY had been dining for once in a way *tête-à-tête*, and she—that is to say, Mrs. Sidney Calvert, a bride of eighteen months' standing—was half lying, half sitting, in the depths of a big, cosy saddle-bag armchair on one side of a bright fire of mixed wood and coal that was burning in one of the most improved imitations of the mediæval fireplace. Her feet—very pretty little feet they were, too, and very daintily shod—were crossed, and poised on the heel of the right one at the corner of the black marble curb.

Dinner was over. The coffee-service and the liqueur-case were on the table, and Mr.

Sidney Calvert, a well-set-up young fellow of about thirty, with a handsome, good-humoured face, which a close observer would have found curiously marred by a chilly glitter in the eyes, and a hardness that was something more than firmness about the mouth, was walking up and down on the opposite side of the table smoking a cigarette.

Mrs. Calvert had just emptied her coffee-cup, and as she put it down on a little three-legged console table behind her, she looked round at her husband, and said—

" Really, Sid, I must say that I can't see why you should do it. Of course it's a very splendid scheme and all that sort of thing, but, surely you, one of the richest men in London, are rich enough to do without it. I'm sure it's wrong, too. What should we think if somebody managed to bottle up the atmosphere and make us pay for every breath we drew? Besides, there must surely be a good deal of risk in deliberately disturbing the economy of nature in such a way. How are you going to get to the Pole, too, to put up your works ? "

" Well," he said, stopping for a moment in his walk and looking thoughtfully at the lighted end of his cigarette, " in the first place, as to the geography, I must remind you that the Magnetic Pole is not the North Pole. It is in Boothia Land, British North America, some fifteen hundred miles south of it. Then, as to the risk, of course one can't do big things like this without taking a certain amount of it ; but, still, I think it will be mostly other people that will have to take it in this case.

" Their risk, you see, will come in when they find that cables and telephones and telegraphs won't work, and that no amount of steam-engine grinding can get up a respect-able amount of electric light—when, in short, all the electric plant of the world loses its value, and can't be set going without buying supplies from the Magnetic Polar Storage Company, or, in other words, from your

humble servant and the few friends that he
will be graciously pleased to let in on the
ground floor. But that is a risk that they
can easily overcome by just paying for it.
Besides, there's no reason why we shouldn't
improve the quality of the commodity. 'Our
Extra Special Greased Lightning!' 'Our
Triple-Concentrated Essence of Electric Fluid,'
and 'Competent Thunderstorms delivered at
the Shortest Notice,' would look very nice in
advertisements, wouldn't they ? "

" Don't you think that's rather a frivolous
way of talking about a scheme which might
end in ruining one of the most important
industries in the world ? " she said, laughing,
in spite of herself, at the idea of delivering
thunderstorms like pounds of butter or
skeins of Berlin wool.

" Well, I'm afraid I can't argue that point
with you, because, you see, you will keep
looking at me while you talk, and that isn't
fair. Anyhow, I'm equally sure that it would
be quite impossible to run any business and

make money out of it on the lines of the
Sermon on the Mount. But, come, here's a
convenient digression for both of us. That's
the Professor, I expect."

"Shall I go?" she said, taking her feet off
the fender.

"Certainly not, unless you wish to," he
said, "or unless you think the scientific
details are going to bore you."

"Oh no, they won't do that," she said.
"The Professor has such a perfectly charming
way of putting them; and, besides, I want to
know all that I can about it."

"Professor Kenyon, sir."

"Ah, good evening, Professor! So sorry
you could not come to dinner," they both
said almost simultaneously as the man of
science walked in.

"My wife and I were just discussing the
ethics of this storage scheme when you came
in," he went on. "Have you anything fresh
to tell us about the practical aspects of it?
I'm afraid she doesn't altogether approve of

it ; but as she is very anxious to hear all about it, I thought you wouldn't mind her making one of the audience."

"On the contrary, I shall be delighted," replied the Professor ; "the more so as it will give me a sympathizer."

" I'm very glad to hear it," said Mrs. Calvert, approvingly.   "I think it will be a very wicked scheme if it succeeds, and a very foolish and expensive one if it fails."

"After which there is, of course, nothing more to be said," laughed her husband, "except for the Professor to give his dispassionate opinion."

" Oh, it shall be dispassionate, I can assure you," he replied, noticing a little emphasis on the word. " The ethics of the matter are no business of mine, nor have I anything to do with its commercial bearings. You have asked me merely to look at technical possibilities and scientific probabilities, and, of course, I don't propose to go beyond these."

He took another sip at a cup of coffee that

Mrs. Calvert had handed him, and went on—

"I've had a long talk with Markovitch this afternoon, and I must confess that I never met a more ingenious man or one who knew as much about magnetism and electricity as he does. His theory that they are the celestial and terrestrial manifestations of the same force, and that what is popularly called electric fluid is developed only at the stage where they become one, is itself quite a stroke of genius, or, at least, it will be if the theory stands the test of experience. His idea of locating the storage works over the Magnetic Pole of the earth is another, and I am bound to confess that, after a very careful examination of his plans and designs, I am distinctly of opinion that, subject to two reservations, he will be able to do what he contemplates."

"And the reservations, what are they?" asked Calvert a trifle eagerly.

"The first is one that it is absolutely necessary to make with regard to all untried schemes, and especially to such a gigantic one as this. Nature, you know, has a way of playing most unexpected pranks with people who take liberties with her. Just at the last moment, when you are on the verge of success, either something that you confidently expect to happen doesn't happen, and there you are left in the lurch ; or the unexpected happens instead, with possibly still more serious consequences. It is utterly impossible to foresee anything of this kind ; but you must clearly understand that if such a thing did occur, it would ruin the enterprise just when you have spent the most money on it—that is to say, at the end and not at the beginning."

"All right," said Calvert, "we'll take that risk. Now, what's the other reservation ?"

"I was going to say something about the immense cost ; but that, I presume, you are prepared for."

Calvert nodded, and he went on—

"Well, that point being disposed of, it remains to be said that it may be very dangerous — I mean to those who live on the spot and will be actually engaged in the work."

"Then, I hope you won't think of going near the place, Sid," interrupted Mrs. Calvert, with a distinct show of wifely authority.

"We'll see about that later, little woman. It's early days yet to get frightened about possibilities. Well, Professor, what was it you were going to say? Any more warnings?"

The Professor's manner stiffened a little as he replied—

"Yes, it is a warning, Mr. Calvert. The fact is, I feel bound to tell you that you propose to interfere very seriously with the distribution of one of the subtlest and least-known forces of Nature, and that the consequences of such an interference might be most disastrous, not only for those engaged in the work, but even the whole hemisphere, and possibly the whole planet.

"On the other hand, I think it is only fair to say that nothing more than a temporary disturbance may take place You may, for instance, give us a series of very violent thunderstorms, with very heavy rains ; or you may abolish thunderstorms and rain altogether until you get to work. Both prospects are within the bounds of possibility, and, at the same time, neither may come to anything."

"Well, I think that quite good enough to gamble on, Professor," said Calvert, who was thoroughly fascinated by the grandeur and magnitude, to say nothing of the dazzling financial aspects, of the scheme. " I am very much obliged to you for putting it so clearly and nicely. Unless something very unexpected happens, we shall get to work on it at once. Just fancy what a glorious thing it will be to play Jove to the nations of the earth, and dole out lightning to them at so much a flash ! "

"Well, I don't want to be ill-natured,"

said Mrs. Calvert, "but I must say that I hope the unexpected *will* happen. I think the whole thing is very wrong, to begin with, and I shouldn't be at all surprised if you blew us all up, or struck us all dead with lightning, or even brought on the Day of Judgment before its time. I think I shall go to Australia while you're doing it."

M

II

A LITTLE more than a year had passed since the after-dinner conversation in the dining-room of Mr. Sidney Calvert's London house. During that time the preparations for the great experiment had been swiftly but secretly carried out. Ship after ship loaded with machinery, fuel, and provisions, and carrying labourers and artificers to the number of some hundreds, had sailed away into the Atlantic, and had come back in ballast and with bare working crews on board of them. Mr. Calvert himself had disappeared and reappeared two or three times, and he neither admitted nor denied any of the various rumours which gradually got into circulation in the city and in the Press.

Some said that it was an expedition to the Pole, and that the machinery consisted partly of improved ice-breakers and newly invented steam-sledges, which were to attack the ice-hummocks after the fashion of battering-rams, and so gradually smooth a road to the Pole. To these little details others added flying machines and navigable balloons.

Others again declared that the object was to plough out the North-West Passage and keep a waterway clear from Baffin's Bay to the Pacific all the year round; and others, somewhat less imaginative, pinned their faith to the founding of a great astronomical and meteorological observatory at the nearest possible point to the Pole, one of the objects of which was to be the determination of the true nature of the Aurora Borealis and the Zodiacal Light.

It was this last hypothesis that Mr. Calvert favoured, as far as he could be said to favour any. There was a vagueness and, at the same time, a distinction about a great scientific expedition which made it possible for him to give a sort of qualified countenance to the rumours without committing himself to anything; but so well had all his precautions been taken that not even a suspicion of the true object of the expedition to Boothia Land had got outside the little circle of those who were in his confidence.

So far, everything had gone as Orloff Markovitch, the Russian Pole, to whose extraordinary genius the inception and working out of the gigantic project were due, had expected and predicted. He himself was in supreme control of the unique and costly, works which had grown up under his constant supervision on that lonely and desolate spot in the far North, where the magnetic needle points straight down to the centre of the world.

Professor Kenyon had paid a couple of visits with Calvert—once at the beginning of the work, and once when it was nearing completion. So far, not the slightest hitch or accident had occurred, and nothing abnormal had been noticed in connection with the earth's electrical phenomena save unusually frequent appearances of the Aurora Borealis and a singular decrease in the deviation of the mariners' compass. Nevertheless, the Professor had politely but firmly refused to remain until the gigantic apparatus was set to work; and Calvert, too, had, with extreme reluctance, yielded to his wife's entreaties, and had come back to England about a month before the initial experiment was to be begun.

The twentieth of March, which was the day fixed for the commencement of operations, came and went, to Mrs. Calvert's intense relief, without anything out of the common happening. Though she knew that over a hundred thousand pounds of her husband's money had been sunk, she found it impossible not to feel a thrill of satisfaction in the hope that Markovitch had made his experiment and failed.

She knew that the great Calvert Company,

which was practically himself, could very well afford it, and she would not have regretted the loss of three times the sum in exchange for the knowledge that Nature was to be allowed to dispose of her electrical forces as seemed good to her. As for her husband, he went about his business as usual, only displaying slight signs of suppressed excitement and anticipation now and then as the weeks went by and nothing happened.

She had not carried out her threat of going to Australia. She had, however, escaped from the rigours of the English spring to a villa near Nice, where she was awaiting the arrival of her second baby—an event which she had found very useful in persuading her husband to stop away from the Magnetic Pole. Calvert himself was so busy with what might be called the home details of the scheme that he had to spend the greater part of his time in London, and could only run over to Nice now and then.

It so happened that Miss Calvert put in an

appearance a few days before she was expected, and therefore while her father was
still in London; and her mother very naturally sent her maid with a telegram to inform
him of the fact and ask him to come over at
once. In about half an hour the maid came
back with the form in her hand, bringing a
message from the telegraph-office that in con-
sequence of some extraordinary accident the
wires had almost ceased to work properly,
and that no messages could be got through
distinctly.

In the rapture of her new motherhood,
Kate Calvert had forgotten all about the
great Storage Scheme, so she sent the maid
back again with the request that the message
should be sent off as soon as possible. Two
hours later she sent again to ask if it had
gone, and the reply came back the wires
had ceased working altogether, and that no
communication by telegraph or telephone was
for the present possible.

Then a terrible fear came to her. The

experiment had been a success, after all, and Markovitch's mysterious engines had been all this time imperceptibly draining the earth of its electric fluid and storing it up in the vast accumulators, which would only yield it back again at the bidding of the Trust which was controlled by her husband.

Still, she was a sensible little woman, and after the first shock she managed, for her baby's sake, to put the fear out of her mind, at any rate, until her husband came. He would be with her in a day or two, and, perhaps, after all, it was only some strange but perfectly natural occurrence which Nature herself would set right in a few hours.

When it got dusk that night, and the electric lights were turned on, it was noticed that they gave an unusually dim and wavering light. The engines were worked to their highest power, and the lines were carefully examined. Nothing could be found wrong with them, but the lights refused to behave as usual, and the most extraordinary feature of the phenomenon was that exactly the same thing was happening in all the electrically lighted cities and towns in the Northern Hemisphere.

By midnight, too, telegraphic and telephonic communication had practically ceased all over the Northern Hemisphere, and the electricians of Europe and America were at their wits' ends to discover any reason for this unheard-of disaster, for such, in sober truth, it would be, unless the apparently suspended force quickly resumed action on its own account. The next morning it was found that, so far as all the marvels of electrical science were concerned, the world had gone back a hundred years.

Then people began to awake to the magnitude of the catastrophe that had befallen the world. Civilized mankind had been suddenly deprived of the services of an obedient slave which it had come to look upon as indispensable.

But there was something even more serious

than this to come. Observers in various parts of the hemisphere remembered that there hadn't been a thunderstorm anywhere for some weeks. Even the regions most frequently visited by them had had none. A most remarkable drought had also set in almost universally.

In addition to this a strange sickness, whose first symptoms were physical lassitude and depression of spirits, which confounded the best medical science of the world, was manifesting itself far and wide, and rapidly assuming the proportions of a universal epidemic.

In the physical world, too, metals were found to be afflicted with an equally incomprehensible disease. Machinery of all sorts got " sick," to use a technical expression, and refused to do its work; and forges and foundries came practically to a standstill for the simple reason that metals seemed to have lost their best properties, and could no longer be worked with as they had been.

Railway accidents and breakdowns on steamers, too, became matters of everyday occurrence, for metals and driving-wheels, piston-rods and propeller-shafts, had acquired an incomprehensible brittleness which only began to be understood when it was discovered that the electrical properties which iron and steel had formerly possessed had almost entirely disappeared.

So far, Calvert had not wavered in his determination to make, as he thought, a colossal amount of money by his usurpation of one of the functions of Nature. To him the calamities, which, it must be confessed, he had deliberately brought upon the world, were only so many arguments for the ultimate success of the stupendous scheme. They were proof positive to the world, or at least they very soon would be, that the Calvert Storage Trust really did control the electricity of the Northern Hemisphere. From the Southern nothing had yet been heard beyond the news that the cables had ceased working.

Hence, as soon as he had demonstrated his power to restore matters to their normal condition, it was obvious that the world would have to pay his price under penalty of having the supply cut off again.

The plan was as simple as it was colossal. Every civilized nation would be called upon to pay a subsidy to the Trust ; and as long as these contributions were regularly and universally paid, Nature would be left to distribute her electrical favours in the ordinary way ; but if one state failed in its payments, orders would be sent to Markovitch to set the apparatus to work, and the supply would be gradually cut off from all. Not the least advantage of this scheme was that it made every nation a watchman over all the others on behalf of the Trust.

It was now getting towards the end of May. On the 1st of June, according to arrangement, Markovitch would stop his engines and permit the vast accumulation of electric fluid in his storage batteries to flow back into its accustomed channels. Then the Trust would issue its prospectus, setting forth the terms upon which it was prepared to permit the nations to enjoy that gift of Nature whose pricelessness the Trust had proved by demonstrating its own ability to corner *it*.

On the evening of May 25th Calvert was sitting in his sumptuous office in Victoria Street, writing by the light of a dozen wax candles in a couple of silver candelabra. The splendid electric-light fittings were of course useless, and for some unexplained but not unknown reason the manufacture of gas had become almost impossible. He had just finished a letter to his wife, telling her to keep up her spirits and fear nothing ; that in a few days the experiment would be over and everything restored to its former condition, shortly after which she would be the wife of a man who would soon be able to buy up all the other millionaires in the world.

As he put the letter into the envelope there was a knock at the door, and Professor Kenyon was announced. Calvert greeted him stiffly and coldly, for he more than half guessed the errand he had come on. There had been two or three heated discussions between them of late, and Calvert knew before the Professor opened his lips that he had come to tell him that he was about to fulfil a threat that he had made a few days before. And this the Professor did tell him in a few dry, quiet words.

"It's no use, Professor," he replied; "you know yourself that I am powerless—as powerless as you are. I have no means of communicating with Markovitch, and the work cannot be stopped until the appointed time. Of course, I am very sorry that the effects of the experiment have been so much more serious than I had anticipated——"

"But you were warned, sir!" the Professor interrupted warmly; "you were warned; and when you saw the effects coming you might have stopped. I wish to God that I had had nothing to do with the infernal business, for

infernal it really is. You have not only
sacrificed the industries and convenience of
nations to your lust of wealth and power.
Thousands of deaths already lie at your door.
This mysterious epidemic, which is neither
more nor less than electrical starvation, is
spreading every day, and human science has
no remedy for it. You alone hold the remedy,
and yet you confess that you are powerless
to apply it before a given date !

" Who are you that you should usurp one of
the functions of the Almighty ?—for that is
really what you are doing. I have kept your
criminal secret too long, and I will keep it no
longer. You have made yourself the enemy
of Society, and Society still has the power to
deal with you—— "

" My dear Professor, that's all nonsense, and
you know it ! " said Calvert, interrupting him
with a contemptuous gesture. " If Society
were to lock me up, it should do without
electricity till I were free. If it hung me, it
would never get any, except on Markovitch's

terms, which would be higher than mine. So you can go and tell your story whenever you please. Meanwhile, you'll excuse me if I remind you that I am rather busy."

Just as the Professor was about to take his leave the door opened, and a boy brought in an envelope deeply edged with black. Calvert turned white to the lips, and his hand trembled as he took it and opened it. It was in his wife's handwriting, and was dated from Nice five days before. He read it through with fixed, staring eyes; then he crushed it into his pocket and strode towards the telephone. He rang the bell furiously, and then he started back with an oath on his lips, remembering that he had made it useless. The sound of a bell brought a clerk into the room immediately.

"Get me a hansom at once!" he almost shouted, and the clerk vanished.

"What is the matter? Where are you going?" asked the Professor.

"Matter? Read that!" he said, thrusting

the crumpled letter into his hand. "My little girl is dead—dead of that accursed sickness which, as you justly say, I have brought on the world; and my wife is down with it, too, and may be dead by this time. That letter's five days' old. My God, what have I done? What can I do? I'd give fifty thousand pounds to get a telegram to Markovitch. Curse him and his infernal scheme! If she dies, I'll go to Boothia Land and kill him! Hullo! What's that? Lightning—by the living God—and thunder!"

As he spoke such a flash of lightning as had never split the skies of London before flared in a huge ragged stream of flame across the zenith, and a roar of thunder such as London's ears had never heard till now shook every house in the vast city to its foundation. Another and another followed in rapid succession, and all through the night and well into the next day there raged, as it was afterwards found, almost all over the whole Northern Hemisphere, such a thunderstorm as had never

N

been known in the world before and never would be again.

With it, too, came hurricanes and cyclones and deluges of rain; and when, after raging for nearly twenty-four hours, it at length ceased convulsing the atmosphere and growled itself away into silence, the first fact that came out of the chaos and desolation that it had left behind it was that the normal electrical conditions of the world had been restored —after which mankind set itself to repair the damage done by the cataclysm and went about its business in the usual way.

The epidemic vanished instantly, and Mrs. Calvert did not die. Nearly six months later a white-haired wreck of a man crawled into her husband's office, and said feebly—

"Don't you know me, Mr. Calvert? I'm Markovitch, or what there is left of him."

"Good God, so you are!" said Calvert. "What has happened to you? Sit down and tell me all about it."

"It is not a long story," said Markovitch,

sitting down and beginning to speak in a thin, trembling voice. " It is not long, but it is very bad. Everything went well at first. All succeeded, as I said it would, and then, I think it was just four days before we should have stopped, it happened."

" What happened ? "

"I don't know. We must have gone too far, or by some means an accidental discharge must have taken place. The whole works suddenly burst into white flame. Everything made of metal melted like tallow, every man in the works died instantly—burnt, you know, to a cinder. I was four or five miles away, with some others, seal shooting. We were all struck down insensible. When I came to myself, I found I was the only one alive.

" Yes, Mr. Calvert, I am the only man that has got back from Boothia alive. The works are gone. There are only some heaps of melted metal lying about on the ice. After that, I don't know what happened. I must have gone mad. It was enough to make a

VI

THE LIZARD

IT is not in the least expected that the general public will believe the statements which will be made in this paper. They are written to catch the eye of Mr. Wilfred Cecil Cording (or Cordy) if he still lives, or in the event of his death to carry some news of his last movements to any of his still existing friends and relations. Further details may be had from me (by any of these interested people) at Poste Restante, Kettlewell, Wharfedale, Yorkshire. My name is M'Cray, and I am sufficiently well known there for letters to be forwarded to wherever I may be at the moment.

The matters in question happened two years ago on the last day of August. I had a small high-ground shoot near Kettlewell, but that morning all the upper parts of the hill were thick with dense mist, and shooting was out of the question. However, I had been going it pretty hard since the twelfth, and was not sorry for an off day, the more so as there was a newly-found cave in the neighbourhood which I was anxious to explore thoroughly. Incidentally I man mad, you know. But some Indians and Eskimos, who used to trade with us, found me wandering about, so they told me, starving and out of my mind, and they took me to the coast. There I got better, and then was picked up by a whaler, and so I got home. That is all. It was very awful, wasn't it?"

Then his face fell forward into his trembling hands, and Calvert saw the tears trickling between his fingers. Suddenly his body slipped gently out of the chair and on to the floor; and when Calvert tried to pick him up, he was dead. And so the secret of the Great Experiment, so far as the world at large was concerned, never got beyond the walls of Mr. Sidney Calvert's cosy dining-room, after all.

"This page was inadvertently missing from the original printing."

may mention that cave-hunting and shooting were then my chief two amusements.

It was my keeper who brought me news to the inn about the impossibility of shooting, and I suggested to him that he should come with me to inspect the cave. He made some sort of excuse — I forget what — and I did not· press the matter further. He was a Kettlewell native, and the dalesmen up there look upon the local caves with more awe than respect. They will not own up to believing in bogles, but I fancy their creed runs that way. I used to have a contempt for their qualms, but latterly I have somehow or other learned to respect them.

I had taken unwilling helpers cave-hunting with me before, and found them such a nuisance that I had made up my mind not to be bothered with them again; so, as I say, I did not press for the keeper's society; but took candles, matches in a bottle, some magnesium wire, a small coil of rope, and a large flask of whisky, and set off alone.

The clouds above were wet, and a fine rain fell persistently. I tramped off along one of the three main roads that lead from the village; but which road it was, had better remain hidden for the present. And in time I got off this road and cut over the moor.

What I was looking for was a fresh scar on the hill side, caused by a roof-fall in one of the countless caves which honeycomb this limestone

district; and although I had got my bearings
pretty accurately, the fog was so thick up there
that I had to take a good dozen casts before I hit
upon the place.

I had not seen it since the 8th of August,
when I first stumbled across it by accident
whilst I was going over the hill to see how the
birds promised for the following twelfth; and I
was a good deal annoyed to find by the boot
marks that quite a lot of people had visited it in
the interval. However, I hoped that the larger
part of these were made by shepherds, and perhaps by my own keepers, and remembering their
qualms, trusted that I might find the interior
still untampered with.

The cave was easy enough to enter. There
was a funnel-shaped slide of peat-earth and mud
and clay to start with, well pitted with boot
marks; and then there was a tumbled wall of
boulders, slanting inwards, down which I crawled
face uppermost till the light behind me dwindled.
The way was getting pretty murky, so I lit up a
candle to avoid accidents, stepped knee-deep into
a lively stream of water, and went briskly ahead.
It was an ordinary enough limestone cave so
far, with inferior stalactites, and a good deal of
wet everywhere. It did not appear to have been
disturbed, and I stepped along cheerfully.

Presently I got a bit of a shock. The roof
above began to droop downwards, slowly but
relentlessly. It seemed as though my way was

soon going to be blocked. However, the water beneath deepened, and so I waded along to inspect as far on as possible. It was a cold job, for the water was icy, but then I am a bit of an enthusiast about cave-hunting, and it takes more than a trifle of discomfort to stop me.

The roof came down and down till I was forced into the water up to my chin, and the air too was none of the best. I was beginning to get disappointed : it looked as if I had got wet through to the bone with freezing cold cave water for no adequate result.

However, there is no accounting for the freaks of caves. Just when I fancied I was at the end of my tether, up went the roof again; I was able to stand erect once more; and a dozen yards further on I came out on to dry rock, and was able to have a rest and a drop of whisky. The roof had quite disappeared to candle-light overhead, so I burned a foot of magnesium wire for a better inspection. It was really a magnificent cave.

But I did not stop to make any accurate measurements or drawings then, and for reasons which will appear, I have not been near to do so since. I was too cold to care for prolonged admiration, and I wanted to (so to speak) annex the whole of the cave's main contours before I took my departure. I was first man in, and wished to be able to describe the whole of my find. There is a certain keen emulation about these matters amongst cave-hunters.

So I walked on over the flat floor of rock, stepping over and through pools, and round boulders, and dodging round stalactites which hung from the unseen roof above, and slipping between slimy palings of stalagmite which sprouted from the floor. And then I came to a regular big subterranean tarn which stretched right across the cavern.

Spaces were big here and the candle did little to show them. It burned brightly enough and that pleased me : one has to be very careful in cave-hunting about foul air, because once overcome by that, it means certain death if one is alone. The air in this cave, however, did not altogether pass muster ; there was something new about it, and anything new in cave smells is always suspicious. It wasn't the smell of peat, or iron, or sandstone, or limestone, or fungus, though all these are common enough in caves ; it was a sort of faint musky smell; and I had got an idea that it was in flavour rather sickly. It is hard to define these things, but that smell, although it might very possibly lead to a new discovery, somehow did not cheer me. In fact at times, when I inhaled a deeper breath of it than usual, it came very near to making my flesh creep.

However, hesitations of this kind are not business. I nipped off another foot of magnesium wire, lit it at the candle, and held the flaming end high above my head. Before me the water of the tarn lay motionless as a mirror of black glass; the sides vignetted away into alleys and bays; the roof was a groined and fretted dome, far overhead; and at the further side was a beach of white tumbled limestone.

I pitched a stone into the black water, and the mirror woke (I was pleased to think) for the first time during a million years into ripples. Yes, it's worth even a year of hard cave-hunting to do a thing like that.

The stone sank with a luscious *plop*. The water was very deep. But I was wet to the neck already, and didn't mind a swim. So with a lump of clay I stuck one candle in my cap; set up a couple more on the dry rock as a light-house to guide my return; lowered myself into the black water, and struck out. The smell of musk oppressed me, and I fancied it was grow-ing more pronounced. So I didn't dawdle. Roughly, I guessed the pool to be some five-and-thirty yards across.

I landed amongst the white, broken limestone on the further side, with a shiver and a scramble, and there was no doubt about the smell of musk now; it was strong enough to make me cough. But when I had stood up, got the candle in my hand again, and peered about through the dark, a thrill came through me as I thought I guessed at the cause. A dozen yards further on amongst the tumbled stone was a broken "cast," where some monstrous uncouth animal had been en-

tombed in the forgotten ages of the past, and
mouldered away and left only the outer shell of
its form and shape. For ages this too had
endured; indeed it had only been violated by
the eroding touch of the water and some earth
tremor within the last few days: perhaps at the
same time that the "slip" was made in the
moor far above, which made an entrance to
the caves.

The "cast" was half full of splintered rubbish,
but even as it was I could see the contour of its
sides in many places, and with care the débris
could be scooped out, and a workman could with
plaster of Paris make an exact model of this beast
which had been lost to the world's knowledge
for so many weary millions of years. It had
been some sort of a lizard or a crocodile, and in
fancy I was beginning to picture its restored
shape posed in the National Museum with my
name underneath as discoverer, when my eye fell
on something amongst the rubble which brought
me to earth with a jar. I stooped and picked it
up. It was a common white-handled penknife,
of the variety sold by stationers for a shilling.
On one side of it was the name of Wilfred Cecil
Cording (or Cordy), scratched apparently with a
nail. The work was neat enough to start with,
but the engraver had wearied with his job; and
the "Cecil" was slip-shod, and the surname too
scratchy to be certain about.

On the hot impulse of the moment, I threw the

knife far from me into the black water, and swore. It is more than a bit unpleasant for an explorer who has made a big discovery to find that he has been forestalled. But since then I have more than once regretted the hard things I said against Cording (if that is his name) in the heat of my first passion. If the man is alive, I apologise to him. If, as I strongly suspect, he came to a horrible end there in the cave, I tender my regrets to his relatives.

I looked upon the cast of the saurian now, with the warmth of discovery quite gone. I was conscious of cold, and moreover the musky smell of the place was vastly unpleasant. And I think I should straightway have gone back to daylight and a change of clothes down in Kettle-well, but for one thing. I seemed somehow or other to trace on the rock beneath me the outline of another cast. It was hazy, as a thing of the kind would be if seen through the medium of sparsely transparent limestone, and by the light of a solitary paraffin-wax candle. I kicked at it petulantly.

Some flakes of stone shelled off, and I distinctly heard a more extensive crack.

I kicked again, harder; with all my might in fact. More flakes shelled away, and there was a little volley of cracks this time. It did not feel like kicking against stone. It was like kicking against something that gave. And I could have sworn that the musky smell increased. I felt

a curious glow coming over me that was part
fright, part excitement, part (I fancy) nausea; but
plucked up my courage, and held my breath, and
kicked again, and again, and again. The laminæ
of limestone flew up in tinkling showers. There
was no doubt about there being something springy
underneath now, and that it was the dead carcass
of another lizard, I hadn't a doubt. Here was
luck; here was a find. Here was I, the discoverer of the body of a prehistoric beast preserved
in the limestone down through all the ages, just
as mammoths have been preserved in Siberian
ice.

The quarrying of my boot-heel was too slow
for me. I stuck my candle by its clay socket to
a rock, and picked up a handy boulder and beat
away the sheets of the stone with that; and all
the time I toiled, the springiness of the carcass
beneath distinctly helped me. The smell of musk
nearly made me sick, but I stuck to the work.
There was no doubt about it now. More than
once I barked my knuckles against the harsh,
scaly skin of the beast itself — against the skin
of this anachronism which ought to have perished
body and bones ten million years ago. I remember wondering whether they would make me a
baronet for the discovery. They do make scientific baronets nowadays for the bigger finds.

Then of a sudden I got a start: I could have
sworn the dead flesh moved beneath me.

But I shouted aloud at myself in contempt.

"Pah!" I said, "ten million years; the ghost is rather stale by this!" And I set to work afresh, beating away the stone which covered the beast from my sight.

But again I got a start, and this time it was a more solid one. After I had delivered my blow and whilst I was raising my weapon for another, a splinter of stone broke away as if pressed up from below, flipped up in the air, and tinkled back to a standstill. My blood chilled, and for a moment the loneliness of that unknown cave oppressed me. But I told myself that I was an old hand; that this was childishness; and, in fact, pulled myself together. I refused to accept the hint. I deliberately put the candle so as to throw a better light, swallowed back my tremors, and battered afresh at the laminated rock.

Twice more I was given warnings and disregarded them in the name of what I was pleased to call cold common reason; but the third time I dropped the battering stone as though it burnt me, and darted back with the most horrible shock of terror which (I make bold to say) any man could endure and still retain his senses.

There was no doubt about it, the beast was actually moving.

Yes, moving and alive. It was writhing, and straining, and struggling to leave its rocky bed, where it had lain quiet through all those countless cycles of time, and I watched it in a very

petrifaction of terror. Its efforts threw up whole
baskets full of splintered stone at a time. I could
see the muscles of its back ripple at each effort.
I could see the exposed part of its body grow in
size every time it wrenched at the walls of that
semi-eternal prison.

Then, as I looked, it doubled up its back like
a bucking horse, and drew out its stumpy head
and long feelers, giving out the while a thin,
small scream like a hurt child; and then with
another effort it pulled out its long tail and stood
upon the débris of the limestone, panting with a
new-found life.

I gazed upon it with a sickly fascination. Its
body was about the bigness of two horses. Its
head was curiously short, but the mouth opened
back almost to the forearm ; and sprouting from
the nose were two enormous feelers, or antennæ,
each at least six feet long, and tipped with fleshy
tendrils like fingers, which opened and shut
tremulously. Its four legs were jointless, and
ended in mere club feet, or callosities; its tail
was long, supple, and fringed on the top with a
saw-like row of scales. In colour it was a bright
grass-green, all except the feelers, which were of
a livid blue. But mere words go poorly for a
description, and the beast was outside the vocabulary of to-day. It conveyed somehow or other a
horrible sense of deformity, which made one
physically ill to look upon it.

But worst of all was the musky smell. That

increased till it became well-nigh unendurable, and though I half-strangled myself to suppress a sound, I had to yield at last and give my feelings vent.

The beast heard me. I could not see that it had any ears, but anyway it distinctly heard me. Worse, it hobbled round clumsily with its jointless legs, and waved its feelers in my direction. I could not make out that it had any eyes; anyway they did not show distinct from the rough skin of its head; its sensitiveness seemed to lie in those fathom-long feelers and in the fleshy fingers which twitched and grappled at the end of them.

Then it opened its great jaws, which hinged, as I said, down by the forearm, and yawned cavernously, and came towards me. It seemed to have no trace of fear or hesitation. It hobbled clumsily on, exhibiting its monstrous deformity in every movement, and preceded always by those hateful feelers, which seemed to be endued with an impish activity.

For a while I stayed in my place, too paralysed by horror by this awful thing I had dragged up from the forgotten dead to move or breathe. But then one of its livid blue feelers — a hard armoured thing like a lobster's — touched me, and the fleshy fingers at the end of it pawed my face and burned me like nettles. I leaped into movement again. The beast was hungry after its fast of ten million years; it was trying to make me its prey; those fearful jaws ——

I turned and ran.

It followed me. In the feeble light of the one solitary candle I could see it following accurately in my track, with the waving feelers and their twitching fingers preceding it. It had pace, too. Its gait, with those clumsy, jointless legs, reminded one of a barrel-bellied sofa suddenly endowed with life, and careering over rough ground. But it distinctly had pace. And what was worse, the pace increased. At first it had the rust of those eternal ages to work out of its cankered joints; but this stiffness passed away; and presently it was following me with a speed equal to my own.

If this huge green beast had shown anger, or eagerness, or any of those things, it would have been less horrible; but it was absolutely unemotional in its hunt, and this helped to paralyse me; and in the end when it.drove me into a *cul de sac* amongst the rocks, I was very near surrendering myself through sheer terror to what seemed the inevitable. I wondered dully whether there had been another beast entombed beside it, and whether that had eaten the man who owned the penknife — Cordy, or Cording, his name was.

But the idea warmed me up. I had a stout knife in my own pocket, and after some fumbling got it out and opened the blade. The feelers with their fringe of fumbling fingers were close to me. I slashed at them viciously,

and felt my knife grate against their armour.
I might as well have hacked at an iron rail.

Still the attempt did me good. There is an
animal love for fighting stowed away in the bottom of all of us somewhere, and mine woke then.
I don't know that I expected to win; but I did
intend to do the largest possible amount of damage before I was caught. I made a rush, stepped
with one foot on the beast's creeping back, and
leaped astern of him; and the beast gave its thin,
small scream, and turned quickly in chase after me.

The pace was getting terrific. We doubled,
and turned, and sprawled, and leapt amongst
the slimy boulders, and every time we came to
close quarters I stabbed at the beast with my
knife, but without ever finding a joint in its
armour. The tough skin gave to the weight of
the blows, it is true, but it was like stabbing
with a stick upon leather.

It was clear, though, that this could not go on.
The beast grew in strength and activity, and
probably in dumb anger, though actually it was
unemotional as ever; but I was every moment
growing more blown, and more bruised, and
more exhausted.

At last I tripped and fell. The beast with
its clumsy waddle shot past me before it could
pull up, and in desperation I threw one arm and
my knees around its grass-green tail, and with
my spare hand drove the knife with the full
of my force into the underneath of its body.

That woke it at last. It writhed, and it plunged, and it bucked with a frenzy that I had never seen before, and its scream grew in piercingness till it was strong as the whistle of a steam engine. But still I hung doggedly on to my place, and planted my vicious blows. The great beast doubled and tried to reach me ; it flung its livid blue feelers backwards in vain efforts : I was beyond its clutch. And then, with my weight still on its back, it gave over dancing about the floor of the cavern, and set off at its hobbling gait directly for the water.

Not till it reached the brink did I slip off ; but I saw it plunge in ; I saw it swim strongly with its tail ; and then I saw it dive and disappear for good.

And what next? I took to the water too, and swam as I had never swam before—swam for dear life, to the opposite side. I knew that if I waited to cool my thoughts, I should never pluck up courage for the attempt. It was then or not at all. It was risk the horrors of that passage, or stay where I was and starve — and be eaten.

How I got across I do not know. How I landed I cannot tell. How I got down the windings of the cave and through that water alley is more than I can say. And whether the beast followed me I do not know either. I got to daylight again somehow, staggering like a drunken man. I struggled down off the moor, and on to the village, and noted how the people

ran from me. At the inn the landlord cried out
as though I had been the plague. It seemed
that the musky smell that I brought with me
was unendurable, though by this time the mere
detail of a smell was far beneath my notice.
But I was stripped from my stinking clothes
and washed and put to bed, and a doctor came
and gave me an opiate ; and when twelve hours
later wakefulness came to me again, I had the
sense to hold my tongue. All the village wanted
to know from whence came that hateful odour
of musk, but I said stupidly I did not know. I
said " I must have fallen into something."

And there the matter ends for the present.
I go no more cave-hunting, and I offer no help
to those who do. But if the man who owned
that white-handled penknife is alive, I should
like to compare experiences with him ; and if,
as I strongly suspect, he is dead, these pages
may be of interest to his relatives. He was not
known in Kettlewell or any of the other villages
where I inquired, but he could very well have
come over the hills from Pateley Bridge way.
Cording was the name scratched on the knife,
or Cordy : I could not be sure which ; and, as I
have said, mine is M'Cray, and I can be heard of
at the Kettlewell Post Office, though I have given
up the shooting on the moor near there. Somehow the air of the district sickens me. There
seems to be a taint in it.

I

THE ROMANCE OF THE
FIRST RADICAL.

————◆◇◆————

A PREHISTORIC APOLOGUE.

" Titius. Le premier qui supprime un abus, comme on
dit, est toujours victime du service qu'il rend.

Un Homme du Peuple. C'est de sa faute ! Pourquoi se
mêlé t'il de ce qui ne le regarde pas."—*Le Prêtre de Nemi.*

THE Devil, according to Dr. Johnson and
other authorities, was the first Whig. History
tells us less about the first Radical—the first
man who rebelled against the despotism of
unintelligible customs, who asserted the rights
of the individual against the claims of the
tribal conscience, and who was eager to see
society organized, off-hand, on what he
thought a rational method. In the absence
of history, we must fall back on that branch
of hypothetics which is known as prehistoric

science. We must reconstruct the Romance of the First Radical from the hints supplied by geology, and by the study of Radicals at large, and of contemporary savages among whom no Radical reformer has yet appeared. In the following little apologue no trait of manners is invented.

The characters of our romance lived shortly after the close of the last glacial epoch in Europe, when the ice had partly withdrawn from the face of the world, and when land and sea had almost assumed their modern proportions. At this period Europe was inhabited by scattered bands of human creatures, who roamed about its surface much as the black fellows used to roam over the Australian continent. The various groups derived their names from various animals and other natural objects, such as the sun, the cabbage, serpents, sardines, crabs, leopards, bears, and hyænas. It is important for our purpose to remember that all the children took their family name from the mother's side. If she were of the Hyæna clan, the children were Hyænas. If the mother were tattooed with the badge of the Serpent, the children were Serpents, and so on. No two persons of the same family name

and crest might marry, on pain of death.
The man of the Bear family who dwelt by
the Mediterranean might not ally himself
with a woman of the Bear clan whose home
was on the shores of the Baltic, and who was
in no way related to him by consanguinity.
These details are dry, but absolutely necessary
to the comprehension of the First Radical's
stormy and melancholy career. We must
also remember that, among the tribes, there
was no fixed or monarchical government.
The little democratic groups were much in-
fluenced by the medicine-men or wizards, who
combined the functions of the modern clergy
and of the medical profession. The old men,
too, had some power; the braves, or warriors,
constituted a turbulent oligarchy; the noisy
outcries of the old women corresponded to
the utterances of an intelligent daily press.
But the real ruler was a body of strange and
despotic customs, the nature of which will
become apparent as we follow the fortunes of
the First Radical.

THE YOUTH OF WHY-WHY.

Why-Why, as our hero was commonly called in the tribe, was born, long before Romulus built his wall, in a cave which may still be observed in the neighbourhood of Mentone. On the warm shores of the Mediterranean, protected from winds by a wall of rock, the group of which Why-Why was the offspring had attained conditions of comparative comfort. The remains of their dinners, many feet deep, still constitute the flooring of the cave, and the tourist, as he pokes the soil with the point of his umbrella, turns up bits of bone, shreds of chipped flint, and other interesting relics. In the big cave lived several little families, all named by the names of their mothers. These ladies had been knocked on the head and dragged home, according to the marriage customs of the period, from places as distant as the modern Marseilles and Genoa. Why-Why, with his little brothers and sisters, were named Serpents, were taught to believe that the serpent was the first ancestor of their race, and that they must never injure any creeping thing. When they were still very

young, the figure of the serpent was tattooed
over their legs and breasts, so that every
member of primitive society who met them
had the advantage of knowing their crest and
highly respectable family name.

The birth of Why-Why was a season of
discomfort and privation. The hill tribe
which lived on the summit of the hill now
known as the Tête du Chien had long been
aware that an addition to the population of
the cave was expected. They had therefore
prepared, according to the invariable etiquette
of these early times, to come down on the cave
people, maltreat the ladies, steal all the property they could lay hands on, and break
whatever proved too heavy to carry. Good
manners, of course, forbade the cave people
to resist this visit, but etiquette permitted
(and in New Caledonia still permits) the
group to bury and hide its portable possessions. Canoes had been brought into the
little creek beneath the cave, to convey the
women and children into a safe retreat, and
the men were just beginning to hide the
spears, bone daggers, flint fish-hooks, mats,
shell razors, nets, and so forth, when Why-
Why gave an early proof of his precocity

by entering the world some time before his arrival was expected.

Instantly all was confusion. The infant, his mother and the other non-combatants of the tribe, were bundled into canoes and paddled, through a tempestuous sea, to the site of the modern Bordighiera. The men who were not with the canoes fled into the depths of the Gorge Saint Louis, which now severs France from Italy. The hill tribe came down at the double, and in a twinkling had "made hay" (to borrow a modern agricultural expression) of all the personal property of the cave dwellers. They tore the nets (the use of which they did not understand), they broke the shell razors, they pouched the opulent store of flint arrowheads and bone daggers, and they tortured to death the pigs, which the cave people had just begun to try to domesticate. After performing these rites, which were perfectly legal—indeed, it would have been gross rudeness to neglect them— the hill people withdrew to their wind-swept home on the Tête du Chien.

Philosophers who believe in the force of early impressions will be tempted to maintain that Why-Why's invincible hatred of established institutions may be traced to these hours of discomfort in which his life began.

The very earliest years of Why-Why, unlike those of Mr. John Stuart Mill, whom in many respects he resembled, were not distinguished by proofs of extraordinary intelligence. He rather promptly, however, showed signs of a sceptical character. Like other sharp children, Why-Why was always asking metaphysical conundrums. Who made men? Who made the sun? Why has the cave-bear such a hoarse voice? Why don't lobsters grow on trees?—he would incessantly demand. In answer to these and similar questions, the mother of Why-Why would tell him stories out of the simple mythology of the tribe. There was quite a store of traditional replies to inquisitive children, replies sanctioned by antiquity and by the authority of the medicine-men, and in this lore Why-Why's mother was deeply versed.

Thus, for example, Why-Why would ask his mother who made men. She would reply that long ago Pund-jel, the first man, made two images of human beings in clay, and stuck on curly bark for hair. He then danced a corroboree round them, and sang a song.

They rose up, and appeared as full-grown men. To this statement, hallowed by imme-morial belief, Why-Why only answered by asking who made Pund-jel. His mother said that Pund-jel came out of a plot of reeds and rushes. Why-Why was silent, but thought in his heart that the whole theory was "bosh-bosh," to use the early reduplicative language of these remote times. Nor could he conceal his doubts about the Deluge and the frog who once drowned all the world. Here is the story of the frog:—"Once, long ago, there was a big frog. He drank himself full of water. He could not get rid of the water. Once he saw a sand-eel dancing on his tail by the sea-shore. It made him laugh so that he burst, and all the water ran out. There was a great flood, and every one was drowned except two or three men and women, who got on an island. Past came the pelican, in a canoe; he took off the men, but wanting to marry the woman, kept her to the last. She wrapped up a log in a 'possum rug to deceive the pelican, and swam to shore and escaped. The pelican was very angry; he began to paint himself white, to show that he was on the war trail, when past came another pelican,

did not like his looks, and killed him with his
beak. That is why pelicans are partly black
and white, if you want to know, my little
dear," said the mother of Why-Why.

Many stories like this were told in the cave,
but they found no credit with Why-Why.
When he was but ten years old, his inquiring
spirit showed itself in the following remarkable manner. He had always been informed
that a serpent was the mother of his race,
and that he must treat serpents with the
greatest reverence. To kill one was sacrilege.
In spite of this, he stole out unobserved and
crushed a viper which had stung his little
brother. He noticed that no harm ensued,
and this encouraged him to commit a still
more daring act. None but the old men
and the warriors were allowed to eat oysters.
It was universally held that if a woman or
a child touched an oyster, the earth would
open and swallow the culprit. Not daunted
by this prevalent belief, Why-Why one day
devoured no less than four dozen oysters,
opening the shells with a flint spear-head,
which he had secreted in his waist-band.
The earth did not open and swallow him
as he had swallowed the oysters, and from

that moment he became suspicious of all the ideas and customs imposed by the old men and wizards.

Two or three touching incidents in domestic life, which occurred when Why-Why was about twelve years old, confirmed him in the dissidence of his dissent, for the first Radical was the first Dissenter. The etiquette of the age (which survives among the Yorubas and other tribes) made it criminal for a woman to see her husband, or even to mention his name. When, therefore, the probable father of Why-Why became weary of supporting his family, he did not need to leave the cave and tramp abroad. He merely ceased to bring in tree-frogs, grubs, roots, and the other supplies which Why-Why's mother was accustomed to find concealed under a large stone in the neighbourhood of the cave.

The poor pious woman, who had always religiously abstained from seeing her lord's face, and from knowing his name, was now reduced to destitution. There was no one to grub up pig-nuts for her, nor to extract insects of an edible sort from beneath the bark of trees. As she could not identify her invisible husband, she was unable to denounce

him to the wizards, who would, for a consideration, have frightened him out of his life or
into the performance of his duty. Thus, even
with the aid of Why-Why, existence became
too laborious for her strength, and she gradually pined away. As she lay in a half-fainting
and almost dying state, Why-Why rushed
out to find the most celebrated local medicine-
man. In half an hour the chief medicine-man
appeared, dressed in the skin of a wolf, tagged
about with bones, skulls, dead lizards, and
other ornaments of his official attire. You
may see a picture very like him in Mr. Catlin's
book about the Mandans. Armed with a
drum and a rattle, he leaped into the presence of the sick woman, uttering unearthly
yells. His benevolent action and "bedside
manner" were in accordance with the medical
science of the time. He merely meant to
frighten away the evil spirit which (according to the received hypothesis) was destroying
the mother of Why-Why. What he succeeded
in doing was to make Why-Why's mother
give a faint scream, after which her jaw fell,
and her eyes grew fixed and staring.

The grief of Why-Why was profound.
Reckless of consequences, he declared, with

impious publicity, that the law which forbade a wife to see her own husband, and the medical science which frightened poor women to death were cruel and ridiculous. As Why-Why (though a promising child) was still under age, little notice was taken of remarks which were attributed to the petulance of youth. But when he went further, and transgressed the law which then forbade a brother to speak to his own sister, on pain of death, the general indignation was no longer repressed. In vain did Why-Why plead that if he neglected his sister no one else would comfort her. His life was spared, but the unfortunate little girl's bones were dug up by a German savant last year, in a condition which makes it only too certain that cannibalism was practised by the early natives of the Mediterranean coast. These incidents then, namely, the neglect of his unknown father, the death of his mother, and the execution of his sister, confirmed Why-Why in the belief that radical social reforms were desirable.

The coming of age of Why-Why was celebrated in the manner usual among primitive people. The ceremonies were not of a character to increase his pleasure in life, nor

his respect for constituted authority. When
he was fourteen years of age, he was pinned,
during his sleep, by four adult braves, who
knocked out his front teeth, shaved his head
with sharp chips of quartzite, cut off the first
joint of his little finger, and daubed his whole
body over with clay They then turned him
loose, imposing on him his name of Why-
Why; 'and when his shaven hair began to
show through the clay daubing, the women
of the tribe washed him, and painted him
black and white. The indignation of Why-
Why may readily be conceived. Why, he
kept asking, should you shave a fellow's head,
knock out his teeth, cut off his little finger,
daub him with clay, and paint him like a
pelican, because he is fourteen years old? To
these radical questions, the braves (who had
all lost their own front teeth) replied, that
this was the custom of their fathers. They
tried to console him, moreover, by pointing
out that now he might eat oysters, and catch
himself a bride from some hostile tribe, or
give his sister in exchange for a wife. This
was little comfort to Why-Why. He had
eaten oysters already without supernatural
punishment, and his sister, as we have seen,

had suffered the extreme penalty of the law.
Nor could our hero persuade himself that to
club and carry off a hostile girl in the dark
was the best way to win a loving wife. He
remained single, and became a great eater of
oysters.

THE MANHOOD OF WHY-WHY.

As time went on our hero developed into
one of the most admired braves of his community. No one was more successful in
battle, and it became almost a proverb that
when Why-Why went on the war-path there
was certain to be meat enough and to spare,
even for the women. Why-Why, though a
Radical, was so far from perfect that he invariably complied with the usages of his time
when they seemed rational and useful. If a
little tattooing on the arm would have saved
men from a horrible disease, he would have
had all the tribe tattooed. He was no bigot.
He kept his word, and paid his debts, for no
one was ever very "advanced" all at once. It
was only when the ceremonious or superstitious ideas of his age and race appeared
to him senseless and mischievous that he

rebelled, or at least hinted his doubts and misgivings. This course of conduct made him feared and hated both by the medicine-men, or clerical wizards, and by the old women of the tribe. They naturally tried to take their revenge upon him in the usual way.

A charge of heresy, of course, could not well be made, for in the infancy of our race there were neither Courts of Arches nor General Assemblies. But it was always possible to accuse Why-Why of malevolent witchcraft. The medicine-men had not long to wait for an opportunity. An old woman died, as old women will, and every one was asking "Who sent the evil spirit that destroyed poor old Dada?" In Why-Why's time no other explanation of natural death by disease or age was entertained. The old woman's grave was dug, and all the wizards intently watched for the first worm or insect that should crawl out of the mould. The head-wizard soon detected a beetle, making, as he alleged, in the direction where Why-Why stood observing the proceedings. The wizard at once denounced our hero as the cause of the old woman's death. To have blenched for a moment would have been ruin. But

O

Why-Why merely lifted his hand, and in a moment a spear flew from it which pinned his denouncer ignominiously to a pine-tree. The funeral of the old woman was promptly converted into a free fight, in which there was more noise than bloodshed. After this event the medicine-men left Why-Why to his own courses, and waited for a chance of turning public opinion against the sceptic.

The conduct of Why-Why was certainly calculated to outrage all conservative feeling. When on the war-path or in the excitement of the chase he had even been known to address a tribesman by his name, as "Old Cow," or "Flying Cloud," or what not, instead of adopting the orthodox nomenclature of the classificatory system, and saying, "Third cousin by the mother's side, thrice removed, will you lend me an arrow?" or whatever it might be. On "tabu-days," once a week, when the rest of the people in the cave were all silent, sedentary, and miserable (from some superstitious feeling which we can no longer understand), Why-Why would walk about whistling, or would chip his flints or set his nets. He ought to have been punished with death, but no one cared to interfere with him,

Instead of dancing at the great "corroborees," or religious ballets of his people, he
would "sit out" with a girl whose sad, romantic history became fatally interwoven with his
own. In vain the medicine-men assured him
that Pund-jel, the great spirit, was angry.
Why-Why was indifferent to the thunder
which was believed to be the voice of Pund-
jel. His behaviour at the funeral of a celebrated brave actually caused what we would
call a reformation in burial ceremonies.

It was usual to lay the corpses of the
famous dead in a cave, where certain of the
tribesmen were sent to watch for forty days
and nights the decaying body. This ghastly
task was made more severe by the difficulty of
obtaining food. Everything that the watchers
were allowed to eat was cooked outside the cave
with complicated ceremonies. If any part of
the ritual was omitted, if a drop or a morsel
were spilled, the whole rite had to be done over
again from the beginning. This was not all.
The chief medicine-man took a small portion
of the meat in a long spoon, and entered the
sepulchral cavern. In the dim light he
approached one of the watchers of the dead,
danced before him, uttered a mysterious

formula of words, and made a shot at the hungry man's mouth with a long spoon. If the shot was straight, if the spoon did not touch the lips or nose or mouth, the watcher made ready to receive a fresh spoonful. But if the attempt failed, if the spoon did not go straight to the mark, the mourners were obliged to wait till all the cooking ceremonies were performed afresh, when the feeding began again.

Now, Why-why was a mourner whom the chief medicine-man was anxious to "spite," as children say, and at the end of three days' watching our hero had not received a morsel of food. The spoon had invariably chanced to miss him. On the fourth night Why-Why entertained his fellow-watchers with a harangue on the imbecility of the whole proceeding. He walked out of the cave, kicked the chief medicine-man into a ravine, seized the pot full of meat, brought it back with him, and made a hearty meal. The other mourners, half dead with fear, expected to see the corpse they were "waking" arise, "girn," and take some horrible revenge. Nothing of the sort occurred, and the burials of the cave dwellers gradually came to be managed in a less irksome way,

THE LOVES OF VERVA AND WHY-WHY.

No man, however intrepid, can offend
with impunity the most sacred laws of
society. Why-Why proved no exception to
this rule. His decline and fall date, we may
almost say, from the hour when he bought
a fair-haired, blue-eyed female child from a
member of a tribe that had wandered out of
the far north. The tribe were about to cook
poor little Verva because her mother was
dead, and she seemed a *bouche inutile.* For
the price of a pair of shell fish-hooks, a bone
dagger, and a bundle of grass-string Why-
Why (who had a tender heart) ransomed the
child. In the cave she lived an unhappy life,
as the other children maltreated and tortured her in the manner peculiar to pitiless
infancy.

Such protection as a man can give to a
child the unlucky little girl received from
Why-Why. The cave people, like most
savages, made it a rule never to punish their
children. Why-Why got into many quarrels
because he would occasionally box the ears
of the mischievous imps who tormented poor
Verva, the fair-haired and blue-eyed captive

from the north. There grew up a kind of friendship between Why-Why and the child. She would follow him with dog-like fidelity and with a stealthy tread when he hunted the red deer in the forests of the Alpine Maritimes. She wove for him a belt of shells, strung on stout fibres of grass. In this belt Why-Why would attend the tribal corroborees, where, as has been said, he was inclined to "sit out" with Verva and watch, rather than join in the grotesque dance performed as worship to the Bear.

As Verva grew older and ceased to be persecuted by the children, she became beautiful in the unadorned manner of that early time. Her friendship with Why-Why began to embarrass the girl, and our hero himself felt a quite unusual shyness when he encountered the captive girl among the pines on the hillside. Both these untutored hearts were strangely stirred, and neither Why-Why nor Verva could imagine wherefore they turned pale or blushed when they met, or even when either heard the other's voice. If Why-Why had not distrusted and indeed detested the chief medicine-man, he would have sought that worthy's professional advice. But he

kept his symptoms to himself, and Verva
also pined in secret.

These artless persons were in love without
knowing it.

It is not surprising that they did not
understand the nature of their complaint, for
probably before Why-Why no one had ever
been in love. Courtship had consisted in
knocking a casual girl on the head in the
dark, and the only marriage ceremony had
been that of capture. Affection on the side
of the bride was out of the question, for, as
we have remarked, she was never allowed so
much as to see her husband's face. Probably
the institution of falling in love has been
evolved in, and has spread from, various
early centres of human existence. Among
the primitive Ligurian races, however, Why-
Why and Verva must be held the inventors,
and, alas! the protomartyrs of the passion.
Love, like murder, "will out," and events
revealed to Why-Why and Verva the true
nature of their sentiments.

It was a considerable exploit of Why-
Why's that brought him and the northern
captive to understand each other. The brother
of Why-Why had died after partaking too

freely of a member of a hostile tribe. The cave people, of course, expected Why-Why to avenge his kinsman. The brother, they said, must have been destroyed by a *boilya* or vampire, and, as somebody must have sent that vampire against the lad, somebody must be speared for it. Such are primitive ideas of medicine and justice. An ordinary brave would have skulked about the dwellings of some neighbouring human groups till he got a chance of knocking over a child or an old woman, after which justice and honour would have been satisfied. But Why-Why declared that, if he must spear somebody, he would spear a man of importance. The forms of a challenge were therefore notched on a piece of stick, which was solemnly carried by heralds to the most renowned brave of a community settled in the neighbourhood of the modern San Remo. This hero might have very reasonably asked, "Why should I spear Why-Why because his brother over-ate himself?" The laws of honour, however (which even at this period had long been established), forbade a gentleman when challenged to discuss the reasonableness of the proceeding.

The champions met on a sandy plain beside a little river near the modern Ventimiglia.
An amphitheatre of rock surrounded them,
and, far beyond, the valley was crowned by
the ancient snow of an Alpine peak. The
tribes of either party gathered in the rocky
amphitheatre, and breathlessly watched the
issue of the battle. Each warrior was
equipped with a shield, a sheaf of spears, and
a heavy, pointed club. At thirty paces distance they began throwing, and the spectators
enjoyed a beautiful exposition of warlike skill.
Both men threw with extreme force and
deadly aim; while each defended himself
cleverly with his shield. The spears were
exhausted, and but one had pierced the thigh
of Why-Why, while his opponent had two
sticking in his neck and left arm.

Then, like two meeting thunder-clouds, the
champions dashed at each other with their
clubs. The sand was whirled up around them
as they spun in the wild dance of battle, and
the clubs rattled incessantly on the heads and
shields. Twice Why-Why was down, but he
rose with wonderful agility, and never dropped
his shield. A third time he stooped beneath
a tremendous whack, but when all seemed

over, grasped a handful of sand, and flung it right in his enemy's eyes. The warrior reeled, blinded and confused, when Why-Why gave point with the club in his antagonist's throat; the blood leaped out, and both fell senseless on the plain.

*   *   *   *   *

When the slow mist cleared from before the eyes of Why-Why he found himself (he was doubtless the first hero of the many heroes who have occupied this romantic position) stretched on a grassy bed, and watched by the blue eyes of Verva. Where were the sand, the stream, the hostile warrior, the crowds of friends and foes? It was Verva's part to explain. The champion of the other tribe had never breathed after he received the club-thrust, and the chief medicine-man had declared that Why-Why was also dead. He had suggested that both champions should be burned in the desolate spot where they lay, that their *boilyas*, or ghosts, might not harm the tribes. The lookers-on had gone to their several and distant caves to fetch fire for the ceremony (they possessed no means of striking a light), and Verva, unnoticed, had lingered beside Why-Why, and laid his bleed-

ing head in her lap. Why-Why had uttered
a groan, and the brave girl dragged him from
the field into a safe retreat among the woods
not far from the stream. Why-Why had been
principally beaten about the head, and his
injuries, therefore, were slight.

After watching the return of the tribesmen,
and hearing the chief medicine-man explain
that Why-Why's body had been carried away
by "the bad black-fellow with a tail who lives
under the earth," Why-Why enjoyed the pleasure of seeing his kinsmen and his foes leave
the place to its natural silence. Then he found
words, and poured forth his heart to Verva.
They must never be sundered—they must be
man and wife! The girl leaned her golden
head on Why-Why's dark shoulder, and
sniffed at him, for kissing was an institution
not yet evolved. She wept. She had a dreadful thing to tell him,—that she could never be
his. "Look at this mark," she said, exposing
the inner side of her arm. Why-Why looked,
shuddered, and turned pale. On Verva's arm
he recognized, almost defaced, the same tattooed badge that wound its sinuous spirals
across his own broad chest and round his
manly legs. *It was the mark of the Serpent!*

Both were Serpents; both, unknown to Why-Why, though not to Verva, bore the same name, the same badge, and, if Why-Why had been a religious man, both would have worshipped the same reptile. Marriage between them then was a thing accursed; man punished it by death. Why-Why bent his head and thought. He remembered all his youth—the murder of his sister for no crime; the killing of the serpent, and how no evil came of it; the eating of the oysters, and how the earth had not opened and swallowed him. His mind was made up. It was absolutely certain that his tribe and Verva's kin had never been within a thousand miles of each other. In a few impassioned words he explained to Verva his faith, his simple creed that a thing was not necessarily wrong because the medicine-men said so, and the tribe believed them. The girl's own character was all trustfulness, and Why-Why was the person she trusted. "Oh, Why-Why, dear," she said blushing (for she had never before ventured to break the tribal rule which forbade calling any one by his name), "Oh, Why-Why, you are *always* right!"

And o'er the hills, and far away
  Beyond their utmost purple rim,
Beyond the night, across the day,
  Through all the world she followed him.

LA MORT WHY-WHY.

Two years had passed like a dream in the
pleasant valley which, in far later ages, the
Romans called Vallis Aurea, and which we
call Vallauris. Here, at a distance of some
thirty miles from the cave and the tribe, dwelt
in fancied concealment Why-Why and Verva.
The clear stream was warbling at their feet,
in the bright blue weather of spring; the
scent of the may blossoms was poured abroad,
and, lying in the hollow of Why-Why's shield,
a pretty little baby with Why-Why's dark
eyes and Verva's golden locks was crowing
to his mother. Why-Why sat beside her,
and was busily making the first European
pipkin with the clay which he had found near
Vallauris. All was peace.

    ＊   ＊   ＊   ＊   ＊

There was a low whizzing sound, something seemed to rush past Why-Why, and
with a scream Verva fell on her face. A
spear had pierced her breast. With a yell

like that of a wounded lion, Why-Why threw himself on the bleeding body of his bride. For many moments he heard no sound but her long, loud and unconscious breathing. He did not mark the yells of his tribesmen, nor feel the spears that rained down on himself, nor see the hideous face of the chief medicine-man peering at his own. Verva ceased to breathe. There was a convulsion, and her limbs were still. Then Why-Why rose. In his right hand was his famous club, "the watcher of the fords;" in his left his shield. These had never lain far from his hand since he fled with Verva.

He knew that the end had come, as he had so often dreamt of it; he knew that he was trapped and taken by his offended tribesmen. His first blow shattered the head of the chief medicine-man. Then he flung himself, all bleeding from the spears, among the press of savages who started from every lentisk bush and tuft of tall flowering heath. They gave back when four of their chief braves had fallen, and Why-Why lacked strength and will to pursue them. He turned and drew Verva's body beneath the rocky wall, and then he faced his enemies. He threw down

shield and club and raised his hands. A
light seemed to shine about his face, and his
first word had a strange tone that caught the
ear and chilled the heart of all who heard him.

"Listen," he said, "for these are the last
words of Why-Why. He came like the
water, and like the wind he goes, he knew not
whence, and he knows not whither. He does
not curse you, for you are that which you are.
But the day will come" (and here Why-Why's
voice grew louder and his eyes burned), "the
day will come when you will no longer be the
slave of things like that dead dog," and here
he pointed to the shapeless face of the slain
medicine-man. "The day will come, when
a man shall speak unto his sister in loving
kindness, and none shall do him wrong. The
day will come when a woman shall unpunished
see the face and name the name of her
husband. As the summers go by you will
not bow down to the hyænas, and the bears,
and worship the adder and the viper. You
will not cut and bruise the bodies of your
young men, or cruelly strike and seize away
women in the darkness. Yes, and the time
will be when a man may love a woman of the
same family name as himself"—but here the

outraged religion of the tribesmen could endure no longer to listen to these wild and blasphemous words. A shower of spears flew out, and Why-Why fell across the body of Verva. His own was "like a marsh full of reeds," said the poet of the tribe, in a song which described these events, "so thick the spears stood in it."

When he was dead, the tribe knew what they had lost in Why-Why. They bore his body, with that of Verva, to the cave; there they laid the lovers—Why-Why crowned with a crown of sea-shells, and with a piece of a rare magical substance (iron) at his side.* Then the tribesmen withdrew from that now holy ground, and built them houses, and forswore the follies of the medicine-men, as Why-Why had prophesied. Many thousands of years later the cave was opened when the railway to Genoa was constructed, and the bones of Why-Why, with the crown, and the fragment of iron, were found where they had been laid by his repentant kinsmen. He had bravely asserted the rights of the individual conscience against the dictates of

* His photograph, thus arrayed, may be purchased at Mentone.

Society; he had lived, and loved, and died,
not in vain. Last April I plucked a rose
beside his cave, and laid it with another
that had blossomed at the door of the last
house which covered the homeless head of
SHELLEY.

The prophecies of Why-Why have been
partially fulfilled. Brothers, if they happen
to be on speaking terms, may certainly speak
to their sisters, though we are still, alas, forbidden to marry the sisters of our deceased
wives. Wives *may* see their husbands, though
in Society, they rarely avail themselves of the
privilege. Young ladies are still forbidden
to call young men at large by their Christian
names; but this tribal law, and survival of
the classificatory system, is rapidly losing its
force. Burials in the savage manner to which
Why-Why objected, will soon, doubtless, be
permitted to conscientious Nonconformists
in the graveyards of the Church of England.
The teeth of boys are still knocked out at
public and private schools, but the ceremony
is neither formal nor universal. Our advance
in liberty is due to an army of forgotten
Radical martyrs of whom we know less than
we do of Mr. Bradlaugh.

THE RED ONE

THERE it was! The abrupt liberation of sound, as he timed it with his watch, Bassett likened to the trump of an archangel. Walls of cities, he meditated, might well fall down before so vast and compelling a summons. For the thousandth time vainly he tried to analyze the tone-quality of that enormous peal that dominated the land far into the strongholds of the surrounding tribes. The mountain gorge which was its source rang to the rising tide of it until it brimmed over and flooded earth and sky and air. With the wantonness of a sick man's fancy, he likened it to the mighty cry of some Titan of the Elder World vexed with misery or wrath. Higher and higher it arose, challenging and demanding in such profounds of volume that it seemed intended for ears beyond the narrow confines of the solar system. There was in it, too, the clamor of protest in that there were no ears to hear and comprehend its utterance.

1

— Such the sick man's fancy. Still he strove
to analyze the sound. Sonorous as thunder was
it, mellow as a golden bell, thin and sweet as a
thrummed taut cord of silver — no; it was none
of these, nor a blend of these. There were no
words nor semblances in his vocabulary and experience with which to describe the totality of that
sound.

Time passed. Minutes merged into quarters
of hours, and quarters of hours into half hours,
and still the sound persisted, ever changing from
its initial vocal impulse yet never receiving fresh
impulse — fading, dimming, dying as enormously
as it had sprung into being. It became a confusion of troubled mutterings and babblings and
colossal whisperings. Slowly it withdrew, sob by
sob, into whatever great bosom had birthed it,
until it whimpered deadly whispers of wrath and
as equally seductive whispers of delight, striving
still to be heard, to convey some cosmic secret,
some understanding of infinite import and value.
It dwindled to a ghost of sound that had lost its
menace and promise, and became a thing that
pulsed on in the sick man's consciousness for
minutes after it had ceased. When he could

hear it no longer, Bassett glanced at his watch. An hour had elapsed ere that archangel's trump had subsided into tonal nothingness.

Was this, then, *his* dark tower? — Bassett pondered, remembering his Browning and gazing at his skeleton-like and fever-wasted hands. And the fancy made him smile — of Childe Roland bearing a slug-horn to his lips with an arm as feeble as his was. Was it months, or years, he asked himself, since he first heard that mysterious call on the beach at Ringmanu? To save himself he could not tell. The long sickness had been most long. In conscious count of time he knew of months, many of them; but he had no way of estimating the long intervals of delirium and stupor. And how fared Captain Bateman of the blackbirder *Nari?* he wondered; and had Captain Bateman's drunken mate died of delirium tremens yet?

From which vain speculations, Bassett turned idly to review all that had occurred since that day on the beach of Ringmanu when he first heard the sound and plunged into the jungle after it. Sagawa had protested. He could see him yet, his queer little monkeyish face eloquent with fear, his back burdened with specimen cases, in his hands Bassett's butterfly net and naturalist's shotgun, as he quavered in Beche de mer English: " Me fella too much fright along bush. Bad fella boy too much stop'm along bush."

Bassett smiled sadly at the recollection. The little New Hanover boy had been frightened, but had proved faithful, following him without hesitancy into the bush in the quest after the source of the wonderful sound. No fire-hollowed tree-trunk, that, throbbing war through the jungle depths, had been Bassett's conclusion. Erroneous had been his next conclusion, namely, that the source or cause could not be more distant than an hour's walk and that he would easily be back by mid-afternoon to be picked up by the *Nari's* whaleboat.

" That big fella noise no good, all the same devil-devil," Sagawa had adjudged. And Sagawa had been right. Had he not had his head hacked off within the day? Bassett shuddered. Without doubt Sagawa had been eaten as well by the bad fella boys too much that stopped along the bush. He could see him, as he had last seen him, stripped of the shotgun

and all the naturalist's gear of his master, lying
on the narrow trail where he had been decapitated barely the moment before. Yes, within a
minute the thing had happened. Within a
minute, looking back, Bassett had seen him
trudging patiently along under his burdens.
Then Bassett's own trouble had come upon him.
He looked at the cruelly healed stumps of the
first and second fingers of his left hand, then
rubbed them softly into the indentation in the
back of his skull. Quick as had been the flash
of the long-handled tomahawk, he had been quick
enough to duck away his head and partially to de-
flect the stroke with his up-flung hand. Two
fingers and a nasty scalp-wound had been the
price he paid for his life. With one barrel of his
ten-gauge shotgun he had blown the life out of
the bushman who had so nearly got him; with
the other barrel he had peppered the bushmen
bending over Sagawa, and had the pleasure of
knowing that the major portion of the charge
had gone into the one who leaped away with
Sagawa's head. Everything had occurred in a
flash. Only himself, the slain bushman, and
what remained of Sagawa, were in the narrow,

wild-pig run of a path. From the dark jungle on either side came no rustle of movement or sound of life. And he had suffered distinct and dreadful shock. For the first time in his life he had killed a human being, and he knew nausea as he contemplated the mess of his handiwork.

Then had begun the chase. He retreated up the pig-run before his hunters, who were between him and the beach. How many there were, he could not guess. There might have been one, or a hundred, for aught he saw of them. That some of them took to the trees and traveled along through the jungle roof he was certain; but at the most he never glimpsed more than an occasional flitting of shadows. No bow-strings twanged that he could hear; but every little while, whence discharged he knew not, tiny arrows whispered past him or struck tree-boles and fluttered to the ground beside him. They were bone-tipped and feather-shafted, and the feathers, torn from the breasts of humming-birds, iridesced like jewels.

Once — and now, after the long lapse of time, he chuckled gleefully at the recollection — he had detected a shadow above him that came to instant rest as he turned his gaze upward. He could make out nothing, but, deciding to chance it, had fired at it a heavy charge of number five shot. Squalling like an infuriated cat, the shadow crashed down through tree-ferns and orchids and thudded upon the earth at his feet, and, still squalling its rage and pain, had sunk its human teeth into the ankle of his stout tramping boot. He, on the other hand, was not idle, and with his free foot had done what reduced the squalling to silence. So inured to savagery had Bassett since become, that he chuckled again with the glee of the recollection.

What a night had followed! Small wonder that he had accumulated such a virulence and variety of fevers, he thought, as he recalled that sleepless night of torment, when the throb of his wounds was as nothing compared with the myriad stings of the mosquitoes. There had been no escaping them, and he had not dared to light a fire. They had literally pumped his body full of poison, so that, with the coming of day, eyes swollen almost shut, he had stumbled blindly on, not caring much when his head should be hacked off and his carcass started on the way of Sagawa's to the cooking fire. Twenty-four hours had made a wreck of him — of mind as well as body. He had scarcely retained his wits at all, so maddened was he by the tremendous inoculation of poison he had received. Several times he fired his shotgun with effect into the shadows that dogged him. Stinging day insects and gnats added to his torment, while his bloody wounds attracted hosts of loathsome flies that clung sluggishly to his flesh and had to be brushed off and crushed off.

Once, in that day, he heard again the wonderful sound, seemingly more distant, but rising imperiously above the nearer war-drums in the bush. Right there was where he had made his mistake. Thinking that he had passed beyond it and that, therefore, it was between him and the beach of Ringmanu, he had worked back toward it when in reality he was penetrating deeper and deeper into the mysterious heart of the unexplored island. That night, crawling in among the twisted roots of a banyan tree, he had slept from exhaustion while the mosquitoes had had their will of him.

Followed days and nights that were vague as

nightmares in his memory. One clear vision he remembered was of suddenly finding himself in the midst of a bush village and watching the old men and children fleeing into the jungle. All had fled but one. From close at hand and above him, a whimpering as of some animal in pain and terror had startled him. And looking up he had seen her — a girl, or young woman, rather, suspended by one arm in the cooking sun. Perhaps for days she had so hung. Her swollen, protruding tongue spoke as much. Still alive, she gazed at him with eyes of terror. Past help, he decided, as he noted the swellings of her legs which advertised that the joints had been crushed and the great bones broken. He resolved to shoot her, and there the vision terminated. He could not remember whether he had or not, any more than could he remember how he chanced to be in that village or how he succeeded in getting away from it.

Many pictures, unrelated, came and went in Bassett's mind as he reviewed that period of his terrible wanderings. He remembered invading another village of a dozen houses and driving all before him with his shotgun save for one old man, too feeble to flee, who spat at him and whined and snarled as he dug open a ground-oven and from amid the hot stones dragged forth a roasted pig that steamed its essence deliciously through its green-leaf wrappings. It was at this place that a wantonness of savagery had seized upon him. Having feasted, ready to depart with a hind quarter of the pig in his hand, he deliberately fired the grass thatch of a house with his burning glass.

But seared deepest of all in Bassett's brain, was the dank and noisome jungle. It actually stank with evil, and it was always twilight. Rarely did a shaft of sunlight penetrate its matted roof a hundred feet overhead. And beneath that roof was an aërial ooze of vegetation, a monstrous, parasitic dripping of decadent life-forms that rooted in death and lived on death. And through all this he drifted, ever pursued by the flitting shadows of the anthropophagi, themselves ghosts of evil that dared not face him in battle but that knew, soon or late, that they would feed on him. Bassett remembered that at the time, in lucid moments, he had likened himself to a wounded bull pursued by plains' coyotes

too cowardly to battle with him for the meat of
him, yet certain of the inevitable end of him when
they would be full gorged.   As the bull's horns
and stamping hoofs kept off the coyotes, so his
shotgun kept off these Solomon Islanders, these
twilight shades of bushmen of the island of
Guadalcanal.

Came the day of the grass lands. Abruptly,
as if cloven by the sword of God in the hand of
God, the jungle terminated.   The edge of it, perpendicular and as black as the infamy of it, was a
hundred feet up and down.   And, beginning at the
edge of it, grew the grass — sweet, soft, tender,
pasture grass that would have delighted the eyes
and beasts of any husbandman and that extended,
on and on, for leagues and leagues of velvet ver-
dure, to the backbone of the great island, the
towering mountain range flung up by some ancient
earth-cataclysm, serrated and gullied but not yet
erased by the erosive tropic rains.   But the grass !
He had crawled into it a dozen yards, buried his
face in it, smelled it, and broken down in a fit of
involuntary weeping.

And, while he wept, the wonderful sound had
pealed forth — if by *peal*, he had often thought

since, an adequate description could be given of
the enunciation of so vast a sound so melting
sweet.   Sweet it was as no sound ever heard.
Vast it was, of so mighty a resonance that it might
have proceeded from some brazen-throated monster.   And yet it called to him across that leagues-
wide savannah, and was like a benediction to his
long-suffering, pain-wracked spirit.

He remembered how he lay there in the grass,
wet-cheeked but no longer sobbing, listening to the
sound and wondering that he had been able to hear
it on the beach of Ringmanu.   Some freak of air
pressures and air currents, he reflected, had made
it possible for the sound to carry so far.   Such
conditions might not happen again in a thousand
days or ten thousand days; but the one day it had
happened had been the day he landed from the
Nari for several hours' collecting.   Especially had
he been in quest of the famed jungle butterfly, a
foot across from wing-tip to wing-tip, as velvet-
dusky of lack of color as was the gloom of the
roof, of such lofty arboreal habits that it resorted
only to the jungle roof and could be brought down
only by a dose of shot.   It was for this purpose

that Sagawa had carried the twenty-gauge shot-gun.

Two days and nights he had spent crawling across that belt of grass land. He had suffered much, but pursuit had ceased at the jungle-edge. And he would have died of thirst had not a heavy thunderstorm revived him on the second day.

And then had come Balatta. In the first shade, where the savannah yielded to the dense mountain jungle, he had collapsed to die. At first she had squealed with delight at sight of his helplessness, and was for beating his brain out with a stout for-est branch. Perhaps it was his very utter help-lessness that had appealed to her, and perhaps it was her human curiosity that made her refrain. At any rate, she had refrained, for he opened his eyes again under the impending blow, and saw her studying him intently. What especially struck her about him were his blue eyes and white skin. Coolly she had squatted on her hams, spat on his arm, and with her finger-tips scrubbed away the dirt of days and nights of muck and jungle that sullied the pristine whiteness of his skin.

And everything about her had struck him espe-

cially, although there was nothing conventional
about her at all.   He laughed weakly at the recollection, for she had been as innocent of garb as
Eve before the fig-leaf adventure.   Squat and lean
at the same time, asymmetrically limbed, string-
muscled as if with lengths of cordage, dirt-caked
from infancy save for casual showers, she was as
unbeautiful a prototype of woman as he, with a
scientist's eye, had ever gazed upon.   Her breasts
advertised at the one time her maturity and youth;
and, if by nothing else, her sex was advertised by
the one article of finery with which she was
adorned, namely a pig's tail, thrust through a hole
in her left ear-lobe.   So lately had the tail been
severed, that its raw end still oozed blood that
dried upon her shoulder like so much candle-drop-
pings.   And her face!   A twisted and wizened
complex of apish features, perforated by upturned,
sky-open, Mongolian nostrils, by a mouth that
sagged from a huge upper-lip and faded precipi-
tately into a retreating chin, and by peering queru-
lous eyes that blinked as blink the eyes of denizens
of monkey-cages.

Not even the water she brought him in a forest-
leaf, and the ancient and half-putrid chunk of roast

pig, could redeem in the slightest the grotesque
hideousness of her. When he had eaten weakly
for a space, he closed his eyes in order not to see
her, although again and again she poked them open
to peer at the blue of them. Then had come the
sound. Nearer, much nearer, he knew it to be;
and he knew equally well, despite the weary way
he had come, that it was still many hours distant.
The effect of it on her had been startling. She
cringed under it, with averted face, moaning and
chattering with fear. But after it had lived its
full life of an hour, he closed his eyes and fell
asleep with Balatta brushing the flies from him.

When he awoke it was night, and she was gone.
But he was aware of renewed strength, and, by
then too thoroughly inoculated by the mosquito
poison to suffer further inflammation, he closed his
eyes and slept an unbroken stretch till sun-up. A
little later Balatta had returned, bringing with her
a half dozen women who, unbeautiful as they were,
were patently not so unbeautiful as she. She evi-
denced by her conduct that she considered him her
find, her property, and the pride she took in showing him off would have been ludicrous had his situation not been so desperate.

Later, after what had been to him a terrible
journey of miles, when he collapsed in front of the
devil-devil house in the shadow of the breadfruit
tree, she had shown very lively ideas on the matter
of retaining possession of him. Ngurn, whom
Bassett was to know afterward as the devil-devil
doctor, priest, or medicine man of the village, had
wanted his head. Others of the grinning and
chattering monkey-men, all as stark of clothes and
bestial of appearance as Balatta, had wanted his
body for the roasting oven. At that time he had
not understood their language, if by *language*
might be dignified the uncouth sounds they made
to represent ideas. But Bassett had thoroughly
understood the matter of debate, especially when
the men pressed and prodded and felt of the flesh
of him as if he were so much commodity in a
butcher's stall.

Balatta had been losing the debate rapidly,
when the accident happened. One of the men,
curiously examining Bassett's shotgun, managed to
cock and pull a trigger. The recoil of the butt
into the pit of the man's stomach had not been the
most sanguinary result, for the charge of shot, at a

distance of a yard, had blown the head of one of
the debaters into nothingness.

Even Balatta joined the others in flight, and, ere
they returned, his senses already reeling from the
oncoming fever-attack, Bassett had regained possession of the gun. Whereupon, although his
teeth chattered with the ague and his swimming
eyes could scarcely see, he held onto his fading
consciousness until he could intimidate the bush-
men with the simple magics of compass, watch,
burning glass, and matches. At the last, with due
emphasis of solemnity and awfulness, he had
killed a young pig with his shotgun and promptly
fainted.

Bassett flexed his arm-muscles in quest of what
possible strength might reside in such weakness,
and dragged himself slowly and totteringly to his
feet. He was shockingly emaciated; yet, during
the various convalescences of the many months of
his long sickness, he had never regained quite the
same degree of strength as this time. What he
feared was another relapse such as he had already
frequently experienced. Without drugs, without
even quinine, he had managed so far to live

through a combination of the most pernicious and most malignant of malarial and black-water fevers. But could he continue to endure? Such was his everlasting query. For, like the genuine scientist he was, he would not be content to die until he had solved the secret of the sound.

Supported by a staff, he staggered the few steps to the devil-devil house where death and Ngurn reigned in gloom. Almost as infamously dark and evil-stinking as the jungle was the devil-devil house — in Bassett's opinion. Yet therein was usually to be found his favorite crony and gossip, Ngurn, always willing for a yarn or a discussion, the while he sat in the ashes of death and in a slow smoke shrewdly revolved curing human heads suspended from the rafters. For, through the months' interval of consciousness of his long sickness, Bassett had mastered the psychological simplicities and lingual difficulties of the language of the tribe of Ngurn and Balatta, and Gngngn — the latter the addle-headed young chief who was ruled by Ngurn, and who, whispered intrigue had it, was the son of Ngurn.

"Will the Red One speak to-day?" Bassett asked, by this time so accustomed to the old man's gruesome occupation as to take even an interest in the progress of the smoke-curing.

With the eye of an expert Ngurn examined the particular head he was at work upon.

" It will be ten days before I can say ' finish,' " he said. " Never has any man fixed heads like these."

Bassett smiled inwardly at the old fellow's reluctance to talk with him of the Red One. It had always been so. Never, by any chance, had Ngurn or any other member of the weird tribe divulged the slightest hint of any physical characteristic of the Red One. Physical the Red One must be, to emit the wonderful sound, and though it was called the Red One, Bassett could not be sure that red represented the color of it. Red enough were the deeds and powers of it, from what abstract clews he had gleaned. Not alone, had Ngurn informed him, was the Red One more bestial powerful than the neighbor tribal gods, ever a-thirst for the red blood of living human sacrifices, but the neighbor gods themselves were sacrificed and tormented before him. He was the god of a dozen allied villages similar to this one, which was the central and commanding village of the federation.

By virtue of the Red One many alien villages had been devastated and even wiped out, the prisoners sacrificed to the Red One. This was true to-day, and it extended back into old history carried down by word of mouth through the generations. When he, Ngurn, had been a young man, the tribes beyond the grass lands had made a war raid. In the counter raid, Ngurn and his fighting folk had made many prisoners. Of children alone over five score living had been bled white before the Red One, and many, many more men and women.

The Thunderer, was another of Ngurn's names for the mysterious deity. Also at times was he called The Loud Shouter, The God-Voiced, The Bird-Throated, The One with the Throat Sweet as the Throat of the Honey-Bird, The Sun Singer, and The Star-Born.

Why The Star-Born? In vain Bassett interrogated Ngurn. According to that old devil-devil doctor, the Red One had always been, just where he was at present, forever singing and thundering his will over men. But Ngurn's father, wrapped in decaying grass-matting and hanging even then over their heads among the smoky rafters of the devil-devil house, had held otherwise. That de-

parted wise one had believed that the Red One
came from out of the starry night, else why — so
his argument had run — had the old and forgotten
ones passed his name down as the Star-Born?
Bassett could not but recognize something cogent
in such argument. But Ngurn affirmed the long
years of his long life, wherein he had gazed upon
many starry nights, yet never had he found a star
on grass land or in jungle depth — and he had
looked for them. True, he had beheld shooting
stars (this in reply to Bassett's contention) ; but
likewise had he beheld the phosphorescence of fun-
goid growths and rotten meat and fireflies on dark
nights, and the flames of wood-fires and of blazing
candle-nuts; yet what were flame and blaze and
glow when they had flamed, and blazed and
glowed? Answer: memories, memories only, of
things which had ceased to be, like memories of
matings accomplished, of feasts forgotten, of desires that were the ghosts of desires, flaring, flaming, burning, yet unrealized in achievement of
easement and satisfaction. Where was the appe-
tite of yesterday? the roasted flesh of the wild
pig the hunter's arrow failed to slay? the maid,
unwed and dead, ere the young man knew her?

A memory was not a star, was Ngurn's contention.   How could a memory be a star?   Further,
after all his long life he still observed the starry
night-sky unaltered.   Never had he noted the absence of a single star from its accustomed place.
Besides, stars were fire, and the Red One was not
fire — which last involuntary betrayal told Bassett
nothing.

"Will the Red One speak to-morrow?" he
queried.

Ngurn shrugged his shoulders as who should
say.

"And the day after? — and the day after
that?" Bassett persisted.

"I would like to have the curing of your head,"
Ngurn changed the subject.   "It is different from
any other head.   No devil-devil has a head like it.
Besides, I would cure it well.   I would take
months and months.   The moons would come and
the moons would go, and the smoke would be very
slow, and I should myself gather the materials for
the curing smoke.   The skin would not wrinkle.
It would be as smooth as your skin now."

He stood up, and from the dim rafters grimed
with the smoking of countless heads, where day

was no more than a gloom, took down a matting-wrapped parcel and began to open it.

"It is a head like yours," he said, "but it is poorly cured."

Bassett had pricked up his ears at the suggestion that it was a white man's head; for he had long since come to accept that these jungle-dwellers, in the midmost center of the great island, had never had intercourse with white men. Certainly he had found them without the almost universal Beche de mer English of the west South Pacific. Nor had they knowledge of tobacco, nor of gunpowder. Their few precious knives, made from lengths of hoop-iron, and their few and more precious toma-hawks, made from cheap trade hatchets, he had surmised they had captured in war from the bush-men of the jungle beyond the grass lands, and that they, in turn, had similarly gained them from the salt water men who fringed the coral beaches of the shore and had contact with the occasional white men.

"The folk in the out beyond do not know how to cure heads," old Ngurn explained, as he drew forth from the filthy matting and placed in Bassett's hands an indubitable white man's head.

Ancient it was beyond question; white it was as the blond hair attested. He could have sworn it once belonged to an Englishman, and to an Englishman of long before by token of the heavy gold circlets still threaded in the withered ear-lobes.

" Now your head . . ." the devil-devil doctor began on his favorite topic.

" I'll tell you what," Bassett interrupted, struck by a new idea. " When I die I'll let you have my head to cure, if, first, you take me to look upon the Red One."

" I will have your head anyway when you are dead," Ngurn rejected the proposition. He added, with the brutal frankness of the savage: " Besides, you have not long to live. You are almost a dead man now. You will grow less strong. In not many months I shall have you here turning and turning in the smoke. It is pleasant, through the long afternoons, to turn the head of one you have known as well as I know you. And I shall talk to you and tell you the many secrets you want to know. Which will not matter, for you will be dead."

"Ngurn," Bassett threatened in sudden anger.

" You know the Baby Thunder in the Iron that is mine." (This was in reference to his all-potent and all-awful shotgun.) " I can kill you any time, and then you will not get my head."

" Just the same, will Gngngn, or some one else of my folk get it," Ngurn complacently assured him. " And just the same will it turn and turn here in the devil-devil house in the smoke. The quicker you slay me with your Baby Thunder, the quicker will your head turn in the smoke."

And Bassett knew he was beaten in the discussion.

What was the Red One? — Bassett asked himself a thousand times in the succeeding week, while he seemed to grow stronger. What was the source of the wonderful sound? What was this Sun Singer, this Star-Born One, this mysterious deity, as bestial-conducted as the black and kinky-headed and monkey-like human beasts who worshiped it, and whose silver-sweet, bull-mouthed singing and commanding he had heard at the taboo distance for so long?

Ngurn had he failed to bribe with the inevitable curing of his head when he was dead. Gngngn, imbecile and chief that he was, was too imbecilic,

too much under the sway of Ngurn, to be considered.   Remained Balatta, who, from the time she
found him and poked his blue eyes open to recru-
descence of her grotesque, female hideousness, had
continued his adorer.   Woman she was, and he
had long known that the only way to win from her
treason to her tribe was through the woman's
heart of her.

Bassett was a fastidious man.   He had never
recovered from the initial horror caused by
Balatta's female awfulness.   Back in England,
even at best, the charm of woman, to him, had
never been robust.   Yet now, resolutely, as only
a man can do who is capable of martyring himself
for the cause of science, he proceeded to violate
all the fineness and delicacy of his nature by making love to the unthinkably disgusting bushwoman.

He shuddered, but with averted face hid his
grimaces and swallowed his gorge as he put his
arm around her dirt-crusted shoulders and felt the
contact of her rancid-oily and kinky hair with his
neck and chin.   But he nearly screamed when she
succumbed to that caress so at the very first of the
courtship and mowed and gibbered and squealed
little, queer, pig-like gurgly noises of delight.   It

was too much. And the next he did in the singular courtship was to take her down to the stream and give her a vigorous scrubbing.

From then on he devoted himself to her like a true swain as frequently and for as long at a time as his will could override his repugnance. But marriage, which she ardently suggested, with due observance of tribal custom, he balked at. Fortunately, taboo rule was strong in the tribe. Thus, Ngurn could never touch bone, or flesh, or hide of crocodile. This had been ordained at his birth. Gngngn was denied ever the touch of woman. Such pollution, did it chance to occur, could be purged only by the death of the offending female. It had happened once, since Bassett's arrival, when a girl of nine, running in play, stumbled and fell against the sacred chief. And the girl-child was seen no more. In whispers, Balatta told Bassett that she had been three days and nights in dying before the Red One. As for Balatta, the bread-fruit was taboo to her. For which Bassett was thankful. The taboo might have been water.

For himself, he fabricated a special taboo. Only could he marry, he explained, when the Southern Cross rode highest in the sky Knowing

his astronomy, he thus gained a reprieve of nearly
nine months; and he was confident that within that
time he would either be dead or escaped to the
coast with full knowledge of the Red One and of
the source of the Red One's wonderful voice.   At
first he had fancied the Red One to be some colossal statue, like Memnon, rendered vocal under
certain temperature conditions of sunlight.   But
when, after a war raid, a batch of prisoners was
brought in and the sacrifice made at night, in the
midst of rain, when the sun could play no part, the
Red One had been more vocal than usual, Bassett
discarded that hypothesis.

In company with Balatta, sometimes with men
and parties of women, the freedom of the jungle
was his for three quadrants of the compass.   But
the fourth quadrant, which contained the Red
One's abiding place, was taboo.   He made more
thorough love to Balatta — also saw to it that she
scrubbed herself more frequently.   Eternal female she was, capable of any treason for the sake
of love.   And, though the sight of her was provocative of nausea and the contact of her provocative
of despair, although he could not escape her awfulness in his dream-haunted nightmares of her, he

nevertheless was aware of the cosmic verity of sex
that animated her and that made her own life of
less value than the happiness of her lover with
whom she hoped to mate. Juliet or Balatta?
Where was the intrinsic difference? The soft and
tender product of ultra-civilization, or her bestial
prototype of a hundred thousand years before her?
— there was no difference.

Bassett was a scientist first, a humanist afterward. In the jungle-heart of Guadalcanal he put
the affair to the test, as in the laboratory he would
have put to the test any chemical reaction. He increased his feigned ardor for the bushwoman, at
the same time increasing the imperiousness of his
will of desire over her to be led to look upon the
Red One face to face. It was the old story, he
recognized, that the woman must pay, and it occurred when the two of them, one day, were catching the unclassified and unnamed little black fish,
an inch long, half-eel and half-scaled, rotund with
salmon-golden roe, that frequented the fresh
water and that were esteemed, raw and whole,
fresh or putrid, a perfect delicacy. Prone in the
muck of the decaying jungle-floor, Balatta threw
herself, clutching his ankles with her hands, kissing

his feet and making slubbery noises that chilled
his backbone up and down again. She begged him
to kill her rather than exact this ultimate love-pay-
ment. She told him of the penalty of breaking the
taboo of the Red One — a week of torture, living,
the details of which she yammered out from her
face in the mire until he realized that he was yet
a tyro in knowledge of the frightfulness the human
was capable of wreaking on the human.

Yet did Bassett insist on having his man's will
satisfied, at the woman's risk, that he might solve
the mystery of the Red One's singing, though she
should die long and horribly and screaming. And
Balatta, being mere woman, yielded. She led him
into the forbidden quadrant. An abrupt mountain, shouldering in from the north to meet a similar intrusion from the south, tormented the stream
in which they had fished into a deep and gloomy
gorge. After a mile along the gorge, the way
plunged sharply upward until they crossed a saddle
of raw limestone which attracted his geologist's
eye. Still climbing, although he paused often
from sheer physical weakness, they scaled forest-
clad heights until they emerged on a naked mesa
or tableland Bassett recognized the stuff of its

composition as black volcanic sand, and knew that
a pocket magnet could have captured a full load of
the sharply angular grains he trod upon.

And then, holding Balatta by the hand and leading her onward, he came to it — a tremendous pit,
obviously artificial, in the heart of the plateau.
Old history, the South Seas Sailing Directions,
scores of remembered data and connotations swift
and furious, surged through his brain. It was
Mendana who had discovered the islands and
named them Solomon's, believing that he had
found that monarch's fabled mines. They had
laughed at the old navigator's child-like credulity;
and yet here stood himself, Bassett, on the rim of
an excavation for all the world like the diamond
pits of South Africa.

But no diamond this that he gazed down upon.
Rather was it a pearl, with the depth of iridescence
of a pearl; but of a size all pearls of earth and
time welded into one, could not have totaled; and
of a color undreamed of any pearl, or of anything
else, for that matter, for it was the color of the
Red One. And the Red One himself Bassett
knew it to be on the instant. A perfect sphere,
fully two hundred feet in diameter, the top of it

was a hundred feet below the level of the rim. He likened the color quality of it to lacquer. Indeed, he took it to be some sort of lacquer, applied by man, but a lacquer too marvelously clever to have been manufactured by the bush-folk. Brighter than bright cherry-red, its richness of color was as if it were red builded upon red. It glowed and iridesced in the sunlight as if gleaming up from underlay under underlay of red.

In vain Balatta strove to dissuade him from descending. She threw herself in the dirt; but, when he continued down the trail that spiraled the pit-wall, she followed, cringing and whimpering her terror. That the red sphere had been dug out as a precious thing, was patent. Considering the paucity of members of the federated twelve villages and their primitive tools and methods, Bassett knew that the toil of a myriad generations could scarcely have made that enormous excavation.

He found the pit bottom carpeted with human bones, among which, battered and defaced, lay village gods of wood and stone. Some, covered with obscene totemic figures and designs, were carved from solid tree trunks forty or fifty feet in length. He noted the absence of the shark and turtle gods, so common among the shore villages, and was amazed at the constant recurrence of the helmet motive. What did these jungle savages of the dark heart of Guadalcanal know of helmets? Had Mendana's men-at-arms worn helmets and penetrated here centuries before? And if not, then whence had the bush-folk caught the motive?

Advancing over the litter of gods and bones, Balatta whimpering at his heels, Bassett entered the shadow of the Red One and passed on under its gigantic overhang until he touched it with his finger-tips. No lacquer that. Nor was the surface smooth as it should have been in the case of lacquer. On the contrary, it was corrugated and pitted, with here and there patches that showed signs of heat and fusing. Also, the substance of it was metal, though unlike any metal or combination of metals he had ever known. As for the color itself, he decided it to be no application. It was the intrinsic color of the metal itself.

He moved his finger-tips, which up to that had merely rested, along the surface, and felt the whole gigantic sphere quicken and live and respond. It was incredible! So light a touch on

so vast a mass! Yet did it quiver under the finger-
tip caress in rhythmic vibrations that became
whisperings and rustlings and mutterings of sound
— but of sound so different; so elusive thin that it
was shimmeringly sibillant; so mellow that it was
maddening sweet, piping like an elfin horn, which
last was just what Bassett decided would be like a
peal from some bell of the gods reaching earth-
ward from across space.

He looked to Balatta with swift questioning;
but the voice of the Red One he had evoked had
flung her face-downward and moaning among the
bones. He returned to contemplation of the
prodigy. Hollow it was, and of no metal known
on earth, was his conclusion. It was right-named
by the ones of old-time as the Star-Born. Only
from the stars could it have come, and no thing of
chance was it. It was a creation of artifice and
mind. Such perfection of form, such hollowness
that it certainly possessed, could not be the result
of mere fortuitousness. A child of intelligences,
remote and unguessable, working corporally in
metals, it indubitably was. He stared at it in
amaze, his brain a racing wild-fire of hypotheses to
account for this far-journeyer who had adventured

the night of space, threaded the stars, and now rose before him and above him, exhumed by patient anthropophagi, pitted and lacquered by its fiery bath in two atmospheres.

But was the color a lacquer of heat upon some familiar metal? Or was it an intrinsic quality of the metal itself? He thrust in the blade-point of his pocket-knife to test the constitution of the stuff. Instantly the entire sphere burst into a mighty whispering, sharp with protest, almost twanging goldenly if a whisper could possibly be considered to twang, rising higher, sinking deeper, the two extremes of the registry of sound threatening to complete the circle and coalesce into the bull-mouthed thundering he had so often heard beyond the taboo distance.

Forgetful of safety, of his own life itself, entranced by the wonder of the unthinkable and unguessable thing, he raised his knife to strike heavily from a long stroke, but was prevented by Balatta. She upreared on her own knees in an agony of terror, clasping his knees and supplicating him to desist In the intensity of her desire to impress him, she put her forearm between her teeth and sank them to the bone.

He scarcely observed her act, although he yielded atomatically to his gentler instincts and withheld the knife-hack. To him, human life had dwarfed to microscopic proportions before this colossal portent of higher life from within the distances of the sidereal universe. As had she been a dog, he kicked the ugly little bushwoman to her feet and compelled her to start with him on an encirclement of the base. Part way around, he encountered horrors. Even, among the others, did he recognize the sun-shriveled remnant of the nine-years girl who had accidentally broken Chief Gngngn's personality taboo. And, among what was left of these that had passed, he encountered what was left of one who had not yet passed. Truly had the bush-folk named themselves into the name of the Red One, seeing in him their own image which they strove to placate and please with such red offerings.

Farther around, always treading the bones and images of humans and gods that constituted the floor of this ancient charnel house of sacrifice, he came upon the device by which the Red One was made to send his call singing thunderingly across the jungle-belts and grass-lands to the far beach of

Ringmanu. Simple and primitive was it as was the
Red One's consummate artifice. A great king-
post, half a hundred feet in length, seasoned by
centuries of superstitious care, carven into dynas-
ties of gods, each superimposed, each helmeted,
each seated in the open mouth of a crocodile, was
slung by ropes, twisted of climbing vegetable para-
sites, from the apex of a tripod of three great
forest trunks, themselves carved into grinning and
grotesque adumbrations of man's modern concepts
of art and god. From the striker king-post, were
suspended ropes of climbers to which men could
apply their strength and direction. Like a battering ram, this king-post could be driven end-onward
against the mighty, red-iridescent sphere.

Here was where Ngurn officiated and functioned
religiously for himself and the twelve tribes under
him. Bassett laughed aloud, almost with mad-
ness, at the thought of this wonderful messenger,
winged with intelligence across space, to fall into a
bushman stronghold and be worshiped by ape-like,
man-eating and head-hunting savages. It was as
if God's Word had fallen into the muck mire of
the abyss underlying the bottom of hell; as if Je-
hovah's Commandments had been presented on

carved stone to the monkeys of the monkey cage
at the Zoo; as if the Sermon on the Mount had
been preached in a roaring bedlam of lunatics.

The slow weeks passed. The nights, by elec-
tion, Bassett spent on the ashen floor of the devil-
devil house, beneath the ever-swinging, slow-curing
heads. His reason for this was that it was taboo
to the lesser sex of woman, and, therefore, a
refuge for him from Balatta, who grew more per-
secutingly and perilously loverly as the Southern
Cross rode higher in the sky and marked the
imminence of her nuptials. His days Bassett
spent in a hammock swung under the shade of
the great breadfruit tree before the devil-devil
house. There were breaks in this program, when,
in the comas of his devastating fever-attacks, he
lay for days and nights in the house of heads.
Ever he struggled to combat the fever, to live, to
continue to live, to grow strong and stronger
against the day when he would be strong enough
to dare the grass-lands and the belted jungle beyond, and win to the beach, and to some labor-
recruiting, black-birding ketch or schooner, and
on to civilization and the men of civilization, to

whom he could give news of the message from other worlds that lay, darkly worshiped by beast-men, in the black heart of Guadalcanal's mid-most center.

On other nights, lying late under the breadfruit tree, Bassett spent long hours watching the slow setting of the western stars beyond the black wall of jungle where it had been thrust back by the clearing for the village. Possessed of more than a cursory knowledge of astronomy, he took a sick man's pleasure in speculating as to the dwellers on the unseen worlds of those incredibly remote suns, to haunt whose houses of light, life came forth, a shy visitant, from the rayless crypts of matter. He could no more apprehend limits to time than bounds to space. No subversive radium specula-tions had shaken his steady scientific faith in the conservation of energy and the indestructibility of matter. Always and forever must there have been stars. And surely, in that cosmic ferment, all must be comparatively alike, comparatively of the same substance, or substances, save for the freaks of the ferment. All must obey, or com-pose, the same laws that ran without infraction through the entire experience of man. Therefore, he argued and agreed, must worlds and life be appanages to all the suns as they were appanages to the particular sun of his own solar system.

Even as he lay here, under the breadfruit tree, an intelligence that stared across the starry gulfs, so must all the universe be exposed to the ceaseless scrutiny of innumerable eyes, like his, though grantedly different, with behind them, by the same token, intelligences that questioned and sought the meaning and the construction of the whole. So reasoning, he felt his soul go forth in kinship with that august company, that multitude whose gaze was forever upon the arras of infinity.

Who were they, what were they, those far distant and superior ones who had bridged the sky with their gigantic, red-iridescent, heaven-singing message? Surely, and long since, had they, too, trod the path on which man had so recently, by the calendar of the cosmos, set his feet. And to be able to send such a message across the pit of space, surely they had reached those heights to which man, in tears and travail and bloody sweat, in darkness and confusion of many counsels, was so slowly struggling. And what were they on

their heights? Had they won Brotherhood? Or
had they learned that the law of love imposed the
penalty of weakness and decay? Was strife, life?
Was the rule of all the universe the pitiless rule
of natural selection? And, and most immediately·
and poignantly, were their far conclusions, their
long-won wisdoms, shut even then in the huge,
metallic heart of the Red One, waiting for the first
earth-man to read? Of one thing he was certain:
No drop of red dew shaken from the lion-mane of
some sun in torment, was the sounding sphere. It
was of design, not chance, and it contained the
speech and wisdom of the stars.

What engines and elements and mastered forces,
what lore and mysteries and destiny-controls,
might be there! Undoubtedly, since so much
could be inclosed in so little a thing as the foundation stone of public building, this enormous
sphere should contain vast histories, profounds of
research achieved beyond man's wildest guesses,
laws and formulæ that, easily mastered, would
make man's life on earth, individual and collective,
spring up from its present mire to inconceivable
heights of purity and power. It was Time's greatest gift to blindfold, insatiable, and sky-aspiring

man. And to him, Bassett, had been vouchsafed the lordly fortune to be the first to receive this message from man's interstellar kin!

No white man, much less no outland man of the other bush-tribes, had gazed upon the Red One and lived. Such the law expounded by Ngurn to Bassett. There was such a thing as blood brotherhood, Bassett, in return, had often argued in the past. But Ngurn had stated solemnly no. Even the blood brotherhood was outside the favor of the Red One. Only a man born within the tribe could look upon the Red One and live. But now, his guilty secret known only to Balatta, whose fear of immolation before the Red One fast-sealed her lips, the situation was different. What he had to do was to recover from the abominable fevers that weakened him and gain to civilization. Then would he lead an expedition back, and, although the entire population of Guadalcanal be destroyed, extract from the heart of the Red One the message of the world from other worlds.

But Bassett's relapses grew more frequent, his brief convalescences less and less vigorous, his periods of coma longer, until he came to know, beyond the last promptings of the optimism inherent in so tremendous a constitution as his own, that he would never live to cross the grass lands, perforate the perilous coast jungle, and reach the sea. He faded as the Southern Cross rose higher in the sky, till even Balatta knew that he would be dead ere the nuptial date determined by his taboo. Ngurn made pilgrimage personally and gathered the smoke materials for the curing of Bassett's head, and to him made proud announcement and exhibition of the artistic perfectness of his intention when Bassett should be dead. As for himself, Bassett was not shocked. Too long and too deeply had life ebbed down in him to bite him with fear of its impending extinction. He continued to persist, alternating periods of unconsciousness with periods of semi-consciousness, dreamy and unreal, in which he idly wondered whether he had ever truly beheld the Red One or whether it was a nightmare fancy of delirium.

Came the day when all mists and cobwebs dissolved, when he found his brain clear as a bell, and took just appraisement of his body's weakness. Neither hand nor foot could he lift. So little control of his body did he have, that he was scarcely aware of possessing one. Lightly indeed

his flesh sat upon his soul, and his soul, in its brief-
ness of clarity, knew by its very clarity, that the
black of cessation was near. He knew the end
was close; knew that in all truth he had with his
eyes beheld the Red One, the messenger between
the worlds; knew that he would never live to carry
that message to the world — that message, for
aught to the contrary, which might already have
waited man's hearing in the heart of Guadalcanal
for ten thousand years. And Bassett stirred with
resolve, calling Ngurn to him, out under the shade
of the breadfruit tree, and with the old devil-devil
doctor discussing the terms and arrangements of
his last life effort, his final adventure in the quick
of the flesh.

" I know the law, O Ngurn," he concluded the
matter. " Whoso is not of the folk may not look
upon the Red One and live. I shall not live anyway. Your young men shall carry me before the
face of the Red One, and I shall look upon him,
and hear his voice, and thereupon die, under your
hand, O Ngurn. Thus will the three things be
satisfied: the law, my desire, and your quicker possession of my head for which all your preparations
wait."

To which Ngurn consented, adding:

" It is better so.   A sick man who cannot get well is foolish to live on for so little a while. Also, is it better for the living that he should go. You have been much in the way of late.   Not but what it was good for me to talk to such a wise one. But for moons of days we have held little talk. Instead, you have taken up room in the house of heads, making noises like a dying pig, or talking much and loudly in your own language which I do not understand.   This has been a confusion to me, for I like to think on the great things of the light and dark as I turn the heads in the smoke.   Your much noise has thus been a disturbance to the long-learning and hatching of the final wisdom that will be mine before I die.   As for you, upon whom the dark has already brooded, it is well that you die now.   And I promise you, in the long days to come when I turn your head in the smoke, no man of the tribe shall come in to disturb us.   And I will tell you many secrets, for I am an old man and very wise, and I shall be adding wisdom to wisdom as I turn your head in the smoke."

So a litter was made, and, borne on the shoulders of half a dozen of the men, Bassett departed on the last little adventure that was to cap the total adventure, for him, of living. With a body of which he was scarcely aware, for even the pain had been exhausted out of it, and with a bright clear brain that accommodated him to a quiet ecstasy of sheer lucidness of thought, he lay back on the lurching litter and watched the fading of the passing world, beholding for the last time the breadfruit tree before the devil-devil house, the dim day beneath the matted jungle roof, the gloomy gorge between the shouldering mountains, the saddle of raw limestone, and the mesa of black, volcanic sand.

Down the spiral path of the pit they bore him, encircling the sheening, glowing Red One that seemed ever imminent to iridesce from color and light into sweet singing and thunder. And over bones and logs of immolated men and gods they bore him, past the horrors of other immolated ones that yet lived, to the three-king-post tripod and the huge king-post striker.

Here Bassett, helped by Ngurn and Balatta, weakly sat up, swaying weakly from the hips, and with clear, unfaltering, all-seeing eyes gazed upon the Red One.

"Once, O Ngurn," he said, not taking his eyes from the sheening, vibrating surface whereon and wherein all the shades of cherry-red played unceasingly, ever a-quiver to change into sound, to become silken rustlings, silvery whisperings, golden thrummings of cords, velvet pipings of elfland, mellow-distances of thunderings.

"I wait," Ngurn prompted after a long pause, the long-handled tomahawk unassumingly ready in his hand.

"Once, O Ngurn," Bassett repeated, "let the Red One speak so that I may see it speak as well as hear it. Then strike, thus, when I raise my hand; for, when I raise my hand, I shall drop my head forward and make place for the stroke at the base of my neck. But, O Ngurn, I, who am about to pass out of the light of day forever, would like to pass with the wonder-voice of the Red One singing greatly in my ears."

"And I promise you that never will a head be so well cured as yours," Ngurn assured him, at the same time signaling the tribesmen to man the propelling ropes suspended from the king-post striker. "Your head shall be my greatest piece of work in the curing of heads."

Bassett smiled quietly to the old one's conceit, as the great carved log, drawn back through two-score feet of space, was released. The next moment he was lost in ecstasy at the abrupt and thunderous liberation of sound. But such thunder! Mellow it was with preciousness of all sounding metals. Archangels spoke in it; it was magnificently beautiful before all other sounds; it was invested with the intelligence of supermen of planets of other suns; it was the voice of God, seducing and commanding to be heard. And — the everlasting miracle of that interstellar metal! Bassett, with his own eyes, saw color and colors transform into sound till the whole visible surface of the vast sphere was a-crawl and titillant and vaporous with what he could not tell was color or was sound. In that moment the interstices of matter were his, and the interfusings and intermating transfusings of matter and force.

Time passed. At the last Bassett was brought back from his ecstasy by an impatient movement of Ngurn. He had quite forgotten the old devil-devil one. A quick flash of fancy brought a husky chuckle into Bassett's throat. His shotgun lay beside him in the litter. All he had to do, muzzle to

head, was press the trigger and blow his head into
nothingness.

But why cheat him? was Bassett's next thought.
Head-hunting, cannibal beast of a human that was
as much ape as human, nevertheless Old Ngurn
had, according to his lights, played squarer than
square. Ngurn was in himself a fore-runner of
ethics and contract, of consideration, and gentle-
ness in man. No, Bassett decided; it would be a
ghastly pity and an act of dishonor to cheat the old
fellow at the last. His head was Ngurn's, and
Ngurn's head to cure it would be.

And Bassett, raising his hand in signal, bending
forward his head as agreed so as to expose cleanly
the articulation to his taut spinal cord, forgot
Balatta, who was merely a woman, a woman
merely and only and undesired. He knew, without seeing, when the razor-edged hatchet rose in
the air behind him. And for that instant, ere the
end, there fell upon Bassett the shadow of the Unknown, a sense of impending marvel of the rending
of walls before the imaginable. Almost, when he
knew the blow had started and just ere the edge
of steel bit the flesh and nerves, it seemed that he
gazed upon the serene face of the Medusa, Truth

— And, simultaneous with the bite of the steel on the onrush of the dark, in a flashing instant of fancy, he saw the vision of his head turning slowly, always turning, in the devil-devil house beside the breadfruit tree.

Waikiki, Honolulu,
May 22, 1916.

BEYOND THE SPECTRUM

THE long-expected crisis was at hand, and the country was on the verge of war. Jingoism was rampant. Japanese laborers were mobbed on the western slope, Japanese students were hazed out of colleges, and Japanese children stoned away from playgrounds. Editorial pages sizzled with burning words of patriotism; pulpits thundered with invocations to the God of battles and prayers for the perishing of the way of the ungodly. Schoolboy companies were formed and paraded with wooden guns; amateur drum-corps beat time to the throbbing of the public pulse; militia regiments, battalions, and separate companies of infantry and artillery, drilled, practiced, and paraded; while the regular army was rushed to the posts and garrisons of the Pacific Coast, and the navy, in three divisions, guarded the Hawaiian Islands, the Philippines, and the larger ports of western America. For Japan had a million trained men, with transports to carry them, battle-ships to guard them; with the choice of objective when she was ready to strike; and she was displaying a national secrecy about her choice especially irritating to molders of public opinion and lovers of fair play. War was not yet declared by either side, though the Japanese minister at Washington had quietly sailed for Europe on private business, and the American minister at Tokio, with several consuls and clerks scattered around the ports of Japan, had left their jobs hurriedly, for reasons connected with their general health. This was the situation when the cabled news from Manila told of the staggering into port of the scout cruiser *Salem* with a steward in command, a stoker at the wheel, the engines in charge of firemen, and the captain, watch-officers, engineers, seamen gunners, and the whole fighting force of the ship stricken with a form of partial blindness which in some cases promised to become total.

The cruiser was temporarily out of commission and her stricken men in the hospital; but by the time the specialists had diagnosed the trouble as amblyopia, from some sudden shock to the optic nerve—followed in cases by complete atrophy, resulting in amaurosis—another ship came into Honolulu in the same predicament. Like the other craft four thousand miles away, her deck force had been stricken suddenly and at night. Still another, a battle-ship, followed into Honolulu, with fully five hundred more or less blind men groping around her decks; and the admiral on the station called in all the outriders by wireless. They came as they could, some hitting sand-bars or shoals on the way, and every one crippled and helpless to fight. The diagnosis was the same—amblyopia, atrophy of the nerve, and incipient amaurosis; which in plain language meant dimness of vision increasing to blindness.

Then came more news from Manila. Ship after ship came in, or was towed in, with fighting force sightless, and the work being done by the "black gang" or the idlers, and each with the same report —the gradual dimming of lights and outlines as the night went on, resulting in partial or total blindness by sunrise. And now it was remarked that those who escaped were the lower-deck workers, those whose duties kept them off the upper deck and away from gunports and deadlights. It was also suggested that the cause was some deadly attribute of the night air in these tropical regions, to which the Americans succumbed; for, so far, the coast division had escaped.

In spite of the efforts of the Government, the Associated Press got the facts, and the newspapers of the country changed the burden of their pronouncements. Bombastic utterances gave way to bitter criticism of an inefficient naval policy that left the ships short of fighters in a crisis. The merging of the line and the staff, which had excited much ridicule when inaugurated, now received more intelligent attention. Former critics of the change not only condoned it, but even demanded the wholesale granting of commissions to skippers and mates of the merchant service; and insisted that surgeons, engineers, paymasters, and chaplains, provided they could still see to box the compass, should be given command of the torpedo craft and smaller scouts. All of which made young Surgeon Metcalf, on waiting orders at San Francisco, smile sweetly and darkly to himself: for his last appointment had been the command of a hospital ship, in which position, though a seaman, navigator, and graduate of Annapolis, he had been made the subject of newspaper ridicule and official controversy, and had even been caricatured as going into battle in a ship armored with court-plaster and armed with hypodermic syringes.

Metcalf had resigned as ensign to take up the study and practice of medicine, but at the beginning of the war scare had returned to his first love, relinquishing a lucrative practice as eye-specialist to tender his services to the Government. And the Government had responded by ranking him with his class as junior lieutenant, and giving him the aforesaid command, which he was glad to be released from. But his classmates and brother officers had not responded so promptly with their welcome, and Metcalf found himself combating a naval etiquette that was nearly as intolerant of him as of other appointees from civil life. It embittered him a little, but he pulled through; for he was a likable young fellow, with a cheery face and pleasant voice, and even the most hide-bound product of Annapolis could not long resist his personality. So he was not entirely barred out of official gossip and speculations, and soon had an opportunity to question some convalescents sent home from Honolulu. All told the same story and described the same symptoms, but one added an extra one. An itching and burning of the face had accompanied the attack, such as is produced by sunburn.

"And where were you that night when it came?" asked Metcalf, eagerly.

"On the bridge with the captain and watch-officers. It was all hands that night. We had made out a curious light to the north'ard, and were trying to find out what it was."

"What kind of a light?"

"Well, it was rather faint, and seemed to be about a mile away. Sometimes it looked red, then green, or yellow, or blue."

"And then it disappeared?"

"Yes, and though we steamed toward it with all the search-lights at work, we never found where it came from."

"What form did it take—a beam or a glow?"

"It wasn't a glow—radiation—and it didn't seem to be a beam. It was an occasional flash, and in this sense was like a radiation—that is, like the spokes of a wheel, each spoke with its own color. But that was at the beginning. In three hours none of us could have distinguished colors."

Metcalf soon had an opportunity to question

others. The first batch of invalid officers arrived from Manila, and these, on being pressed, admitted that they had seen colored lights at the beginning of the night. These, Metcalf remarked, were watch-officers, whose business was to look for strange lights and investigate them. But one of them added this factor to the problem.

"And it was curious about Brainard, the most useless and utterly incompetent man ever graduated. He was so near-sighted that he couldn't see the end of his nose without glasses; but it was he that took the ship in, with the rest of us eating with our fingers and asking our way to the sick-bay."

"And Brainard wore his glasses that night?" asked Metcalf.

"Yes; he couldn't see without them. It reminds me of Nydia, the blind girl who piloted a bunch out of Pompeii because she was used to the darkness. Still, Brainard is hardly a parallel."

"Were his glasses the ordinary kind, or pebbles?"

"Don't know. Which are the cheapest? That's the kind."

"The ordinary kind."

"Well, he had the ordinary kind—like himself. And he'll get special promotion. Oh, Lord! He'll be jumped up a dozen numbers."

"Well," said Metcalf, mysteriously, "perhaps not. Just wait."

Metcalf kept his counsel, and in two weeks there came Japan's declaration of war in a short curt note to the Powers at Washington. Next day the papers burned with news, cabled *via* St. Petersburg and London, of the sailing of the Japanese fleet from its home station, but for where was not given—in all probability either the Philippines or the Hawaiian Islands. But when, next day, a torpedo-boat came into San Francisco in command of the cook, with his mess-boy at the wheel, conservatism went to the dogs, and bounties were offered for enlistment at the various navy-yards, while commissions were made out as fast as they could be signed, and given to any applicant who could even pretend to a knowledge of yachts.   And Surgeon George Metcalf, with the rank of junior lieutenant, was ordered to the torpedo-boat above mentioned, and with him as executive officer a young graduate of the academy, Ensign Smith, who with the enthusiasm and courage of youth combined the mediocrity of inexperience and the full share of the service prejudice against civilians.

This prejudice remained in full force, unmodified by the desperate situation of the country; and the unstricken young officers filling subordinate positions on the big craft, while congratulating him, openly denied his moral right to a command that others had earned a better right to by remaining in the service; and the old jokes, jibes, and satirical references to syringes and sticking-plaster whirled about his head as he went to and fro, fitting out his boat and laying in supplies.   And when they learned—from young Mr. Smith—that among these supplies was a large assortment of plain-glass spectacles, of no magnifying power whatever, the ridicule was unanimous and heartfelt; even the newspapers taking up the case from the old standpoint and admitting that the line ought to be drawn at lunatics and foolish people. But Lieutenant Metcalf smiled and went quietly ahead, asking for and receiving orders to scout.

He received them the more readily, as all the scouts in the squadron, including the torpedo-flotilla and two battle-ships, had come in with blinded crews. Their stories were the same—they had all seen the mysterious colored lights, had gone blind, and a few had felt the itching and tingling of sunburn.   And the admiral gleaned one crew of whole men from the fleet, and with it manned his best ship, the *Delaware*.

Metcalf went to sea, and was no sooner outside the Golden Gate than he opened his case of spectacles, and scandalized all hands, even his executive officer, by stern and explicit orders to wear them night and day, putting on a pair himself as an example.

A few of the men attested good eyesight; but this made no difference, he explained. They were to wear them or take the consequences, and as the first man to take the consequences was Mr. Smith, whom he sent to his room for twenty-four hours for appearing on deck without them five minutes afterward, the men concluded that he was in earnest and obeyed the order, though with smiles and silent ridicule. Another explicit command they received more readily: to watch out for curious looking craft, and for small objects such as floating casks, capsized tubs or boats, et cetera. And this brought results 'the day after the penitent Smith was released. They sighted a craft without spars steaming along on the horizon and ran down to her. She was a sealer, the skipper explained, when hailed, homeward bound under the auxiliary. She had been on fire, but the cause of the fire was a mystery. A few days before a strange-looking vessel had passed them, a mile away. She was a whaleback sort of a hull, with sloping ends, without spars or funnels, only a slim pole amidships, and near its base a projection that looked like a liner's crow's-nest. While they watched, their foremast burst into flames, and while they were rigging their hose the mainmast caught fire. Before this latter was well under way they noticed a round hole burnt deeply into the mast, of about four inches diameter. Next, the topsides caught fire, and they had barely saved their craft, letting their masts burn to do so.

"Was it a bright, sunshiny day?" asked Metcalf.

" Sure. Four days ago. He was heading about sou'west, and going slow."

" Anything happen to your eyesight? "

" Say—yes. One of my men's gone stone blind. Thinks he must have looked squarely at the sun when he thought he was looking at the fire up aloft."

" It wasn't the sun. Keep him in utter darkness for a week at least. He'll get well. What was your position when you met that fellow? "

" About six hundred miles due nor'west from here."

" All right. Look out for Japanese craft. War is declared."

Metcalf plotted a new course, designed to intercept that of the mysterious craft, and went on, so elated by the news he had heard that he took his gossipy young executive into his confidence.

" Mr. Smith," he said, " that sealer described one of the new seagoing submersibles of the Japanese, did he not? "

" Yes, sir, I think he did—a larger submarine, without any conning-tower and the old-fashioned periscope. They have seven thousand miles' cruising radius, enough to cross the Pacific."

By asking questions of various craft, and by diligent use of a telescope, Metcalf found his quarry three days later—a log-like object on the horizon, with the slim white pole amidships and the excrescence near its base.

" Wait till I get his bearing by compass," said Metcalf to his chief officer, " then we'll smoke up our specs and run down on him. Signal him by the International Code to put out his light, and to heave to, or we'll sink him."

Mr. Smith bowed to his superior, found the numbers of these commands in the code book, and with a string of small flags at the signal-yard, and every man aboard viewing the world darkly through a smoky film, the torpedo-boat approached the stranger at thirty knots. But there was no blinding glare of light in their eyes, and when they were within a hundred yards of the submersible, Metcalf removed his glasses for a moment's distinct vision. Head and shoulders out of a hatch near the tube was a man waving a white handkerchief. He rang the stopping bells.

" He surrenders, Mr. Smith," he said, joyously, " and without firing a torpedo! "

He examined the man through the telescope and laughed.

" I know him," he said. Then funneling his hands, he hailed:

" Do you surrender to the United States of America? "

" I surrender," answered the man. " I am helpless."

" Then come aboard without arms. I'll send a boat."

A small dinghy-like boat was dispatched, and it returned with the man, a Japanese in lieutenant's uniform, whose beady eyes twinkled in alarm as Metcalf greeted him.

" Well, Saiksi, you perfected it, didn't you?— my invisible search-light, that I hadn't money to go on with."

The Jap's eyes sought the deck, then resumed their Asiatic steadiness.

" Metcalf—this you," he said, " in command? I investigated and heard you had resigned to become a doctor."

" But I came back to the service, Saiksi. Thanks to you and your light—my light, rather—I am in command here in place of men you blinded. Saiksi, you deserve no consideration from me, in spite of our rooming together at Annapolis. You took—I don't say stole—my invention, and turned it against the country that educated you. You, or your *confrères*, did this before a declaration of war. You are a pirate, and I could string you up to my signal-yard and escape criticism."

"I was under orders from my superiors, Captain Metcalf."

"They shall answer to mine. You shall answer to me. How many boats have you equipped with my light?"

"There are but three. It is very expensive."

"One for our Philippine squadron, one for the Hawaiian, and one for the coast. You overdid things, Saiksi. If you hadn't set fire to that sealer the other day, I might not have found you. It was a senseless piece of work that did you no good. Oh, you are a sweet character! How do you get your ultraviolet rays—by filtration or prismatic dispersion?"

"By filtration."

"Saiksi, you're a liar as well as a thief. The colored lights you use to attract attention are the discarded rays of the spectrum. No wonder you investigated me before you dared flash such a decoy! Well, I'm back in the navy, and I've been investigating you. As soon as I heard of the first symptom of sunburn, I knew it was caused by the ultraviolet rays, the same as from the sun; and I knew that nothing but my light could produce those rays at night time. And as a physician I knew what I did not know as an inventor—the swift amblyopia that follows the impact of this light on the retina. As a physician, too, I can inform you that your country has not permanently blinded a single American seaman or officer. The effects wear off."

The Jap gazed stolidly before him while Metcalf delivered himself of this, but did not reply.

" Where is the Japanese fleet bound? " he asked, sternly.

" I do not know."

" And would not tell, whether you knew or not. But you said you were helpless. What has happened to you? You can tell that."

" A simple thing, Captain Metcalf. My supply of oil leaked away, and my engines must work slowly. Your signal was useless; I could not have turned on the light."

" You have answered the first question. You are far from home without a mother-ship, or she would have found you and furnished oil before this. You have come thus far expecting the fleet to follow and strike a helpless coast before your supplies ran out."

Again the Jap's eyes dropped in confusion, and Metcalf went on.

" I can refurnish your boat with oil, my engineer and my men can handle her, and I can easily learn to manipulate your—or shall I say *our*—invisible search-light. Hail your craft in English and order all hands on deck unarmed, ready for transshipment to this boat. I shall join your fleet myself."

A man was lounging in the hatchway of the submersible, and this man Saiksi hailed.

" Ae-hai, ae-hai, Matsu. We surrender. We are prisoner. Call up all men onto the deck. Leave arms behind. We are prisoner."

They mustered eighteen in all, and in half an hour they were ironed in a row along the stanchioned rail of the torpedo-boat.

" You, too, Saiksi," said Metcalf, coming toward him with a pair of jingling handcuffs.

" Is it not customary, Captain Metcalf," said the Jap, " to parole a surrendered commander? "

" Not the surrendered commander of a craft that uses new and deadly weapons of war unknown to her adversary, and before the declaration of war. Hold up your hands. You're going into irons with your men. All Japs look alike to me, now."

So Lieutenant Saiksi, of the Japanese navy, was ironed beside his cook and meekly sat down on the deck. With the difference of dress, they really did look alike.

Metcalf had thirty men in his crew. With the assistance of his engineer, a man of mechanics, he picked eighteen of this crew and took them and a barrel of oil aboard the submersible. Then for three days the two craft lay together, while the engineer and the men familiarized themselves with her internal economy—the torpedo-tubes, gasoline-engines, storage-batteries, and motors; and the vast system of pipes, valves, and wires that gave life and action to the boat—and while Metcalf experimented with the mysterious search-light attached to the periscope tube invented by himself, but perfected by others. Part of his investigation extended into the night. Externally, the light resembled a huge cup about two feet in diameter, with a thick disk fitted around it in a vertical plane. This disk he removed; then, hailing Smith to rig his fire-hose and get off the deck, he descended the hatchway and turned on the light, viewing its effects through the periscope. This, be it known, is merely a perpendicular, non-magnifying telescope that, by means of a reflector at its upper end, gives a view of the seascape when a submarine boat is submerged. And in the eyepiece at its base Metcalf beheld a thin thread of light, of such dazzling brilliancy as to momentarily blind him, stretch over the sea; but he put on his smoked glasses and turned the apparatus, tube and all, until the thin pencil of light touched the end of the torpedo-boat's signal-yard. He did not need to bring the two-inch beam to a focus; it burst into flame and he quickly

shut off the light and shouted to Smith to put out
the fire—which Smith promptly did, with open comment to his handful of men on this destruction of
Government property.

"Good enough!" he said to Smith, when next they
met. "Now if I'm any good I'll give the Japs a
taste of their own medicine."

"Take me along, captain," burst out Smith in
sudden surrender. "I don't understand all this, but
I want to be in it."

"No, Mr. Smith. The chief might do your work,
but I doubt that you could do his. I need him; so
you can take the prisoners home. You will undoubtedly retain command."

"Very good, sir," answered the disappointed
youngster, trying to conceal his chagrin.

"I don't want you to feel badly about it. I know
how you all felt toward me. But I'm on a roving
commission. I have no wireless apparatus and no
definite instructions. I've been lampooned and ridi-
culed in the papers, and I'm going to give them my
answer—that is, as I said, if I'm any good. If I'm
not I'll be sunk."

So when the engineer had announced his mastery
of his part of the problem, and that there was
enough of gasoline to cruise for two weeks longer,
Smith departed with the torpedo-boat, and Metcalf
began his search for the expected fleet.

It was more by good luck than by any possible
calculation that Metcalf finally found the fleet. A
steamer out of San Francisco reported that it had not
been heard from, and one bound in from Honolulu
said that it was not far behind—in fact had sent a
shot or two. Metcalf shut off gasoline, waited a day,
and saw the smoke on the horizon. Then he submerged to the awash condition, which in this boat just
floated the search-light out of water; and thus

balanced, neither floating nor sinking nor rolling, but rising and falling with the long pulsing of the ground-swell, he watched through the periscope the approach of the enemy.

It was an impressive spectacle, and to a citizen of a threatened country a disquieting one. Nine high-sided battle-ships of ten-gun type—nine floating forts, each one, unopposed, able to reduce to smoking ruin a city out of sight of its gunners; each one impregnable to the shell fire of any fortification in the world, and to the impact of the heaviest torpedo yet constructed—they came silently along in line-ahead formation, like Indians on a trail. There were no compromises in this fleet. Like the intermediate batteries of the ships themselves, cruisers had been eliminated and it consisted of extremes, battle-ships, and torpedo-boats, the latter far to the rear. But between the two were half a dozen colliers, repair, and supply ships.

Night came down before they were near enough for operations, and Metcalf turned on his invisible light, expanding the beam to embrace the fleet in its light, and moved the boat to a position about a mile away from its path. It was a weird picture now showing in the periscope each gray ship a bluish-green against a background of black marked here and there by the green crest of a breaking sea. Within Metcalf's reach were the levers, cranks, and worms that governed the action of the periscope and the light; just before him were the vertical and horizontal steering-wheels; under these a self-illuminating compass, and at his ear a system of push-buttons, speaking-tubes, and telegraph-dials that put him in communication with every man on the boat, each one of whom had his part to play at the proper moment, but not one of whom could see or know the result. The work to be done was in Metcalf's hands and brain, and, considering its potentiality, it was a most undramatic performance.

He waited until the leading flag-ship was within half a mile of being abreast; then, turning on a hanging electric bulb, he held it close to the eyepiece of the periscope, knowing that the light would go up the tube through the lenses and be visible to the fleet. And in a moment he heard faintly through the steel walls the sound transmitted by the sea of a bugle-call to quarters. He shut off the bulb, watched a wandering shaft of light from the flag-ship seeking him, then contracted his own invisible beam to a diameter of about three feet, to fall upon the flag-ship, and played it back and forth, seeking gun ports and apertures and groups of men, painting all with that blinding light that they could not see, nor immediately sense. There was nothing to indicate that he had succeeded; the faces of the different groups were still turned his way, and the futile search-light still wandered around, unable to bring to their view the white tube with its cup-like base.

Still waving the wandering beam of white light, the flag-ship passed on, bringing along the second in line, and again Metcalf turned on his bulb. He heard her bugle-call, and saw, in varied shades of green, the twinkling red and blue lights of her masthead signals, received from the flag-ship and passed down the line. And again he played that green disk of deadly light upon the faces of her crew. This ship, too, was seeking him with her search-light, and soon, from the whole nine, a moving network of brilliant beams flashed and scintillated across the sky; but not one settled upon the cause of their disquiet.

Ship after ship passed on, each with its bugle-call to quarters, each with its muster of all hands to meet the unknown emergency—the menace on a hostile coast of a faint white light on the port beam—but not one firing a shot or shell; there was nothing to fire at. And with the passing of the last of the nine Metcalf listened to a snapping and a buzzing overhead that told of the burning out of the carbons in the light.

"Good work for the expenditure," he murmured, wearily. "Let's see—two carbons and about twenty amperes of current, against nine ships at ten millions apiece. Well, we'll soon know whether or not it worked."

While an electrician rigged new carbons he rested his eyes and his brain; for the mental and physical strain had been severe. Then he played the light upon the colliers and supply ships as they charged by, disposing of them in the same manner, and looked for other craft of larger menace. But there were none, except the torpedo contingent, and these he decided to leave alone. There were fifteen of them, each as speedy and as easily handled as his own craft; and already, apprised by the signaled instructions from ahead, they were spreading out into a fan-like formation, and coming on, nearly abreast.

"The jig's up, chief," he called through a tube to the engineer. "We'll get forty feet down until the mosquitoes get by. I'd like to take a chance at them but there are too many. We'd get torpedoed, surely."

Down went the diving rudder, and, with a kick ahead of the engine, the submersible shot under, heading on a course across the path of the fleet, and in half an hour came to the surface. There was nothing in sight, close by, either through the periscope or by direct vision, and Metcalf decided to make for San Francisco and report.

It was a wise decision, for at daylight he was floundering in a heavy sea and a howling gale from the northwest that soon forced him to submerge again for comfort. Before doing so, however, he enjoyed one good look at the Japanese fleet, far ahead and to port. The line of formation was broken, staggered, and disordered; and, though the big ships were making good weather of it, they were steering badly, and on one of them, half-way to the signal-yard, was the appeal for help that ships of all nations use and recognize—the ensign, upside-down. Under the lee of each ship was snuggled a torpedo-boat, plunging, rolling, and swamped by the breaking seas that even the mighty bulk to windward could not protect them from. And even as Metcalf looked, one twisted in two, her after funnels pointing to port, her forward to starboard, and in ten seconds had disappeared.

Metcalf submerged and went on at lesser speed, but in comfort and safety. Through the periscope he saw one after the other of the torpedo-craft give up the fight they were not designed for, and ship after ship hoist that silent prayer for help. They yawed badly, but in some manner or other managed to follow the flag-ship, which, alone of that armada, steered fairly well. She kept on the course for the Golden Gate.

Even submerged Metcalf outran the fleet before noon, and at night had dropped it, entering the Golden Gate before daylight, still submerged, not only on account of the troublesome turmoil on the surface, but to avoid the equally troublesome scrutiny of the forts, whose search-lights might have caught him had he presented more to their view than a slim tube painted white. Avoiding the mines, he picked his way carefully up to the man-of-war anchorage, and arose to the surface, alongside the *Delaware*, now the flag-ship, as the light of day crept upward in the eastern sky.

"We knew they were on the coast," said the admiral, a little later, when Metcalf had made his report on the quarter-deck of the *Delaware*. " But about this light? Are you sure of all this? Why, if it's so, the President will rank you over us all. Mr. Smith came in with the prisoners, but he said nothing of an invisible light—only of a strong search-light with which you set fire to the signal-yard."

" I did not tell him all, admiral," answered Metcalf, a little hurt at the persistence of the feeling. " But I'm satisfied now. That fleet is coming on with incompetents on the bridge."

" Well, we'll soon know. I've only one ship, but it's my business to get out and defend the United States against invaders, and as soon as I can steam against this gale and sea I'll go. And I'll want you, too. I'm short-handed."

" Thank you, sir. I shall be glad to be with you. But wouldn't you like to examine the light? "

" Most certainly," said the admiral; and, accompanied by his staff, he followed Metcalf aboard the submersible.

" It is very simple," explained Metcalf, showing a rough diagram he had sketched. " You see he has used my system of reflectors about as I designed it. The focus of one curve coincides with the focus of the next, and the result is a thin beam containing nearly all the radiations of the arc."

" Very simple," remarked the admiral, dryly. " Very simple indeed. But, admitting this strong beam of light that, as you say, could set fire to that sealer, and be invisible in sunshine, how about the beam that is invisible by night? That is what I am wondering about."

" Here, sir," removing the thick disk from around the light. " This contains the prisms, which refract the beam entirely around the lamp; and disperse it into the seven colors of the spectrum. All the visible light is cut out, leaving only the ultraviolet rays, and these travel as fast and as far, and return by reflection, as though accompanied by the visible rays."

" But how can you see it? " asked an officer. " How is the ship it is directed at made visible? "

" By fluorescence," answered Metcalf. " The observer is the periscope itself. Any of the various fluorescing substances placed in the focus of the object-glass, or at the optical image in front of the eyepiece, will show the picture in the color peculiar to the fluorescing material. The color does not matter."

" More simple still," laughed the admiral. " But how about the colored lights they saw? "

" Simply the discarded light of the spectrum. By removing this cover on the disk, the different colored rays shoot up. That was to attract attention. I used only white light through the periscope."

" And it was this invisible light that blinded so many men, which in your hands blinded the crews of the Japanese? " asked the admiral.

" Yes, sir. The ultraviolet rays are beneficial as a germicide, but are deadly if too strong."

" Lieutenant Metcalf," said the admiral, seriously, " your future in the service is secure. I apologize for laughing at you; but now that it's over and you've won, tell us about the spectacles."

" Why, admiral," responded Metcalf, " that was the simplest proposition of all. The whole apparatus —prisms, periscope, lenses, and the fluorescing screen—are made of rock crystal, which is permeable to the ultraviolet light. But common glass, of which spectacles are made, is opaque to it. That is why near-sighted men escaped the blindness."

" Then, unless the Japs are near-sighted, I expect an easy time when I go out."

But the admiral did not need to go out and fight. Those nine big battle-ships that Japan had struggled for years to obtain, and the auxiliary fleet of supply and repair ships to keep them in life and health away from home, caught on a lee shore in a hurricane against which the mighty *Delaware* could not steam to sea, piled up one by one on the sands below Fort Point; and, each with a white flag replacing the reversed ensign, surrendered to the transport or collier sent out to take off the survivors.

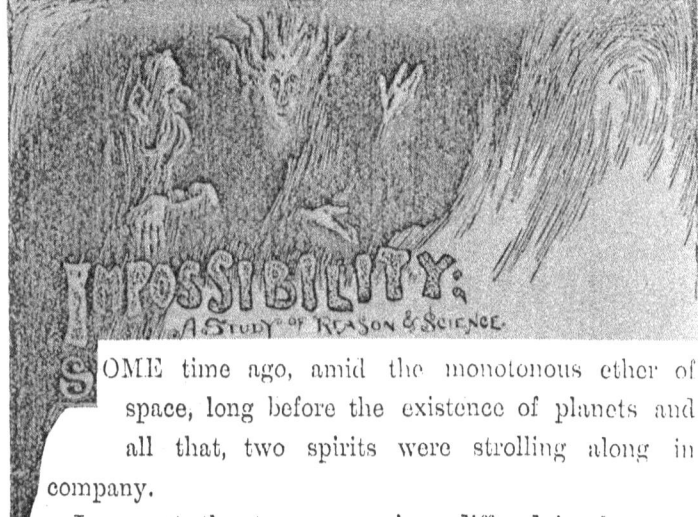

IMPOSSIBILITY:

A STUDY OF REASON & SCIENCE.

SOME time ago, amid the monotonous ether of space, long before the existence of planets and all that, two spirits were strolling along in company.

In aspect the two companions differed in the most pronounced way. On the brow of the one, who might have passed for the elder, appeared the cold and passionless calculation of science; the eye was deeply reflective, but unemotional; the demeanour was grave and deliberate. We may as well speak of this spirit henceforth as William.

The younger, whom we will call James, was of a very different stamp; for in him the quick and well-opened eye, the mobile brow and mouth, and the eager voice, denoted enthusiasm and enterprise.

As we have remarked, the scene was monotonous; it is easily described: stretching away and away for ever in every direction spread space and utter and intense darkness.

What wonder, then, that surrounded by so dull and uninteresting a monotony, living through an indefinite period enlivened by no divisions of time, the soul of James should have cast about within itself for some recreative topic, some object on which to expend its imaginative energies. In truth James was a dreamer—a wild and fantastic dreamer, if you will. Sitting alone, perhaps, for an uninterrupted period of many cycles, he would follow with ever more impetuous mental footsteps the bewildering paths of inventive speculation. In the midst of that dull void he would conceive the existence of many things; he would fill space with entities, psychical and even material.

For many æons the fear of ridicule had deterred him from breathing a word of all these phantasies to his more severe and calculating companion; for to William's cold and precise reason, that which existed was all that ever could exist; and stern philosophic argument had convinced him that space and darkness were everything which could ever possibly be designed or executed.

This was no grudging conservatism, nor prejudice against new things. No, he had worked the matter out in the light of pure reason and scientific argument, and he *knew*.

"William," said James, at length, impelled by an impulse which he could no longer restrain, yet with the detectable nervousness and hesitation of one who fears reproach or ridicule—"William, has it never crossed your mind that the surroundings of our existence are a little—that is, a trifle— monotonous and samey?"

He stopped suddenly, abashed, and fidgeted uncomfortably from foot to foot, as the keen eye of the other, wide with astonishment was fixed upon him.

"I fear I do not catch your meaning, James," at length replied the wiser spirit.

James flushed uncomfortably; but he had committed himself too far for further hesitation. "Might there not exist," he went on, though still nervously, "something beyond mere space and darkness?"

"Something beyond?" repeated the sage, "certainly not: that is impossible. Space and darkness, as Science and Reason conclusively prove, are the only conditions which

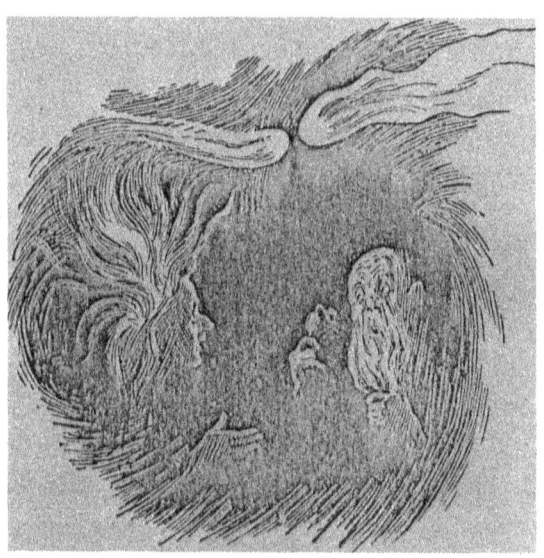

"'Ah, just so,' said William witheringly."

can ever possibly exist. What phantasy is this for which you hanker? Give details."

"Well—why could there not be worlds about?" asked James, bold in very desperation.

"Foolish boy!" replied the philosopher. "Do you think I have not often thought this thing out for myself? Were I to adduce the thousand and one scientific reasons which prove the impossibility of the existence of worlds, you could not follow me. Tell me, whence would you fetch your materials with which to manufacture these worlds?"

James was silent. "How many worlds would you like to have, in your foolishness?" asked the sage.

"Well," said James humbly, "I was thinking of two— one of them all on fire, to give light to the other; and the other for working purposes."

"Ah, just so," said William witheringly. "Of course, it has never occurred to you that the two would dash together by mutual attraction and become one? How about that?"

"Well—I would have a whole lot of them, to keep one another in position—"

"Ah," said William, "and they would all dash together at a common centre, however many you had."

"Hum—that *is* a bother," said James disappointedly; "because I was going to put all manner of things on my worlds."

"As what?" asked the philosopher, with a crushing grin.

"Well, I thought of human beings among other things— when I say human beings I mean something alive and able to move about when supported on anything solid, such as a world; and endowed with a certain amount of reason, and able to express his thoughts, and subject to emotions and proclivities—mostly evil, of course, and—"

"Well now, look here," said William magnanimously, "let us suppose that you have got over all the insurmount- able obstacles in the way of keeping your human beings alive; let us wildly take it for granted that they have not been crushed between your worlds, nor by the attraction of their own—that they can move upon its surface (which, of course, any attraction sufficient to keep them from tumbling

off would inevit-
ably prevent their
doing)—that they
are not shrivelled
up by the heat
generated by the
friction of your
large mass of
material pressing
towards its
centre, not
frozen, nor other-
wise instantly
destroyed (which
they assuredly
would be): let us
suppose this initial absurdity, and
go ahead. What do you intend
your human beings to do? By
the way, I pass over the sublime
humour of anything *having to be
supported on something solid* as a
necessary condition of moving
about! That is a peculiar sort of
motion—but let that pass. Well?"

The sage took up an easy
attitude with an air of resignation,
and prepared to listen.

"Before you begin," said he,
parenthetically, "I can tell you
in a word what your beings would

"They would fight and ex-
terminate each other."

C

do first—and last. They would fight and exterminate each other, and there would be an end of them."

"No," said James, "I believe they would increase in numbers and gradually become less savage, and begin to invent things—"

"Oh, *they* are to invent things as well as you. And I suppose the things they invented would invent other things, and so on?"

"No, they would invent inanimate objects, such as weapons."

"Oh yes," said William nastily, "I have no doubt they would invent weapons; *that* would help them towards extermination."

"Yes, of course they would invent weapons first; but, as they grew less savage—"

"Hum—inventing weapons is a peculiar mode of making oneself less savage!"

"Why, the weapons, as they became more deadly and efficient, would get so capable of exterminating them that they would prove the actual means of civilizing and rendering them more humane—"

"What does 'humane' mean?"

"It is the same as human, that is, kind, sympathizing, benevolent, mild, compassionate, tender, merciful."

"Oh, indeed!" said William; "pray go on."

"By degrees their relations one with another would become more polished and pleasant; a stranger would not necessarily be a foe—"

"Hold hard a moment," said the sage; "how many of these human beings do you propose to have in your world? —some dozens?"

" Many millions."

" *Millions!!* But are they all to be precisely alike, so that one could not be distinguished from another? If that were so, everything would be utter confusion."

" Of course. That would never do. Each must necessarily have his individuality."

" Varying the positions of the parts."

" That would be somewhat difficult when it came to *millions*," said William. " Of course, while you confined yourself to dozens, one might be spherical, another cubical, a third triangular, a fourth oval, and so forth—"

" Bless your soul!" said James. " My human beings are not to be in the form of geometrical figures! Each would have a body, two legs, two arms, a head, and so on."

" Oh! I see; and you will differentiate between them by varying the positions of these parts—now placing the head at the end of one leg, now of the other; now putting the legs and arms at the four corners, and the head in the middle—and so forth."

"Not in the least. The positions of all parts would be relatively identical in all cases."

"Now James, when you talk something distantly approaching reason I can bear with you (by an effort); but if you are going to talk such childish nonsense as this, I must leave you. You speak of *millions* of individuals whose general conformation is practically unvaried; and yet each one is to be individually recognizable—how?"

"He would have to carry a document."

" Why—why, by minor peculiarities, I suppose—"

" ' Minor peculiarities ! '   Then one of your beings would, on meeting another, have to institute a thorough and minute examination of him from end to end in order to discover one of these ' minor peculiarities ' by which to identify him.   He would hardly be able to *remember* the minor peculiarities of all the other millions of individuals, and would therefore have to carry a document whereon each of them was set down.   Very practical !   Now let us work it out : This scroll of his has to contain, let us say, ten million different signs, with the name of the owner attached.   Perhaps you will tell me how he is going to carry this scroll, which would certainly weigh some hundred-weights ?   Then, granting he could carry it, he is to sit down and wade through ten millions of signs in order to identify his friend or enemy. This would occupy a considerable time."

The younger spirit looked crestfallen.

" Lists of identifying peculiarities set up."

" I must admit you rather have me there ! " he said rue-
fully. " I see there *would* be a difficulty about recognition.
Perhaps there might be lists of identifying peculiarities set
up at various points of the world, so that everybody could
meet there and—"

" Pooh ! " said William, " get on to some other absurdity.
I can't see what, save fighting, you would give your creatures
to do."

" Oh, they would have to gain their living—to provide for
themselves."

" Food ? "

" Yes, they could only keep alive by consuming period-
ically something which would nourish their frames."

" Whence would they obtain it ? "

" From the material of which their world was made."

" Oh, I see—your beings would gradually increase in
numbers, and at the same time eat away the world they
were clinging to, until, in course of time, there would be
no world left to cling to at all ? But I suppose you would
lengthen the thing out—they would only eat at intervals of
an æon or so ? "

" No ; I was thinking of several times a day."

The sage burst into a loud laugh, which rolled away for
ever through space.

" What ? Creatures whose frames would begin to dwindle
away unless they ate *every few hours ?* Why, they would
be able to think of nothing else ! Eating would take up all
their time ! They would barely have leisure to kill one
another between meals ! "

" No, there's something in that," said poor James.

" Besides, you have invented beings possessing something

like intelligence. Have you provided that intelligence simply to be used in eating?"

"Oh no; but—"

"Well, they certainly wouldn't have a chance of using it for any other purpose. Are they to live to eat?"

"Oh no—only to eat to live."

"As soon as they had used their intelligence in eating, what is the next thing they would turn it to?"

"To—er—well, I suppose to finding something for the next meal," said poor James hopelessly.

"Precisely," said William. "You do not propose a very high standard of achievement for your beings! I presume all these inventions you talk about would have eating as their ultimate object? The best thing for them would be to invent something to render the necessity of eating less frequent; something which would do all the eating for them, and set them at liberty to attempt something else. What inventions were you thinking of?"

"Well—the electric telegraph, for instance; an apparatus to enable persons to talk to others long distances off."

"But your people wouldn't have time to talk to those at hand even—they would have to eat. By the way, what do you do with your beings when they die?"

"Eating would take
✗ up all their time."

" They become part of the world they lived on."

" Oh ! and the others eat them ? Ah, very nice ! I really begin to like your human beings. Their tastes are so pleasant ! Go on."

" Well, as they progressed in civilization they would make laws."

" What for ? "

" To govern themselves by."

" Govern themselves by. But they could govern themselves without laws. What would they want laws for ? "

" To prevent their doing wrong," said James.

" But if they were inclined to do right they would not need laws to keep them from doing wrong ; while, if they were inclined to do wrong, they would not make such laws. Besides, the necessity of such laws seems to imply that the majority of your humans would have a leaning towards evildoing ? "

" Yes, that would be so."

" Then who would make, and enforce, those laws ? "

" The better inclined minority."

" What horrid nonsense ! The majority would not let them ! No ; obviously the majority would make the laws ; and the majority being inclined towards evil, the laws would be for the propagation of evil-doing. If the majority of your humans were inclined to swindle their neighbours, the laws would be made in favour of swindlers."

Poor James hastily ran over a few of the laws he had conceived, and expressed a wish to change the conversation.

" Look here, my poor boy," said William, rising, " don't muddle your head with any more of these preposterous plans. Science and Reason utterly confute the possibility of such a world as you describe. To begin with, the world itself could not exist for five minutes; then your people couldn't live in it if it did ; if they could live, they couldn't move ; if they could live and move, they would not have a moment for anything but eating ; they could not recognize or identify each other; and so on, and so on. The whole thing is a farrago of hopeless and impossible bosh, and couldn't hold water for a single instant. Science and Reason prove it ! "

As the spirits ceased, we turned to our newspaper and read the following words :—

"*The North American Review* lately described the recent successful experiments carried on in the Far West of America to produce rain by explosives. The result was complete success. . . . This article was followed by a paper by Professor Newcombe, in which he demonstrates conclusively that it is absolutely impossible to make rain in any such way."

LOVE AND A TRIANGLE

A MAN came out of a mine, looked about him, inhaled the odor from the stunted spruce trees, looked up at the clear skies, then called to a boy idling in a shed at a little distance from the mine buildings, telling him to bring out the horse and buckboard. The name of the man who had issued from the mine was Julius Corbett, and he was a civil engineer. Furthermore, he was a capitalist.

He was an intelligent looking man of about thirty-five, and a resolute looking one, this Julius Corbett, and as he stood waiting for the buckboard, was rather worth seeing, vigorous of frame, clear of eye and bronzed by a summer's work in a wild country. The shaft from which he had just emerged was that of a silver mine not five miles distant from Black Bay, one of the inlets of the northern shore of Lake Superior, and was a most valuable property, of which he was chief owner. He had inherited from an uncle in Canada a few hundred acres of land in this region, but had scarcely considered it worthy the payment of its slight taxes until some of the many attempts at mining in the region had proved successful, and it was shown that the famous Silver Islet, worked out years ago in Lake Superior, was not the only repository thereabouts of the precious metal. Then he had abandoned for a time the practice of his profession— he had an office in Chicago—and had visited what he referred to lightly as his "British possessions." He had found rich indications, had called in mining experts, who confirmed all he had imagined, and had returned to Chicago and organized a company. There was a monotonous success to the undertaking, much at variance with the story of ordinary mining enterprises. Corbett had become a very rich man within two years; he was worth more than a million, and was becoming richer daily. He was, seemingly, a person much to be envied, and would not himself, on the day here referred to, have denied such imputation, for he was in love with an exceedingly sweet and clever girl, and knew that he had won this same charming creature's heart. They were plighted to each other, but the date of their marriage was not yet fixed. He had closed up his business at the mine for the season, and was now about to hasten to Chicago, where the day of so much importance to him would be fixed upon and the sum of his good fortune soon made complete. This was in September, 1898.

It was not a commonplace girl whom Corbett was to marry. On the contrary, she was exceptionally gifted, and a young woman whose cleverness had been supplemented by an elaborate education. There was, however, running through her character a vein of what might be called emotionalism. The habit of concentration, acquired through study, seemed rather to intensify this quality than otherwise. Perhaps it made even greater her love for Corbett, but it was destined to perplex him.

In September the air is crisp along the route from Black Bay to Duluth, and from that through fair Wisconsin to Chicago, and Corbett's spirits were high throughout the journey. Was he not to meet Nell Morrison, in his estimation the sweetest girl on earth? Was he not soon to possess her entirely and for a permanency? He made mental pictures of the meeting, and drifted into a lover's mood of planning. Out of his wealth what a home he would provide for her, and how he would gratify her gentle whims! Even her astronomical fancy, Vassar-born, should become his own, and there should be an observatory to the house. He had a weakness for astronomy himself, and was glad his wife-to-be had the same taste intensified. They would study the heavens together from a heaven of their own. What was wealth good for anyhow, save to make happy those we love?

The train sped on, and Chicago was reached, and very soon thereafter was reached the home of the Morrisons. Corbett could not complain of his reception. The one creature was there, sweet as a woman may be, eager to meet him, and with ten-

derness and steadfastness shown in every line of
her pretty face. They spent a charming day and
evening together, and he was content. Once or
twice, just for a moment, the young woman seemed
abstracted, but it was only for a moment, and the
lover thought little of the circumstance. He was
happy when he bade her good-night. "To-morrow, dear," said he, "we will talk of something of
greatest importance to me, of importance to us
both." She blushed and made no answer for a
second. Then she said that she loved him dearly,
and that what affected one must affect the other,
and that she would look for him very early in the
afternoon. He went to his hotel buoyant. The
world was good to him.

When Corbett called at the Morrison mansion
the next day he entered without ringing, as was his
habit, and went straight to the library, expecting
to find Nell there. He was disappointed, but there
were traces of her recent presence. There was an
astronomical map open upon the table, and books
and reviews lay all about, each open, with a marker
indicating a special page. A little glove lay
upon the floor, and Corbett picked it up and
kissed it.

He summoned a servant and sent upstairs to
announce his presence; then turned instinctively to
note what branch of her favorite study was now
attracting his sweetheart's attention. He picked
up one of the open reviews, an old one by the

way, and read a marked passage there. It was
as follows:

"It will always be more difficult for us to communicate with the people of Mars than to receive
signals from them, because of our position and
phases. It is the nocturnal terrestrial hemisphere
that is turned toward the planet Mars in the periods
when we approach most nearly to it, and it shows
us in full its lighted hemisphere. But communication is possible."

He looked at a map. It was a great chart of the
surface of Mars, made by the famous Italian Schiaparelli, and he looked at more of the reviews and
found ever the same subject considered in the
marked articles. All related to Mars. He was
puzzled but delighted. "The dear girl has a
hobby," he thought. "Well, she shall enjoy it to
the utmost."

Nelly entered the room. Her face lighted up
with pleasure when she met her fiancé, but assumed
a more thoughtful look as she saw what he was
reading. She welcomed him, though, as kindly as
any lover could demand, and he, of course, was
joyously content. "Still an astronomer, I see," he
said, "and apparently with a specialty. I see
nothing but Mars, all Mars! Have you become
infatuated with a single planet, to the neglect of all
the others? I like it, though. We will study
Mars together."

Her face brightened. "I am so glad!" she said.

"I have studied nothing else for months. It has been so almost from the day you left us. And it is not Mars alone I am studying; it is the great problem of communication with the people there. Oh, Julius, it is possible, and the idea is something wonderful! Just think what would follow! It would be the beginning of an understanding between reasoning creatures of the whole universe!"

He said that it was something wonderful, indeed, maybe only a dream, but a very fascinating one.

"Oh, it is no dream," she answered. "It is a glorious possibility. Why, just think of it, we know, positively know, that Mars is inhabited. Think of what has been discovered. It was perceived years ago that Mars was intersected by canals, evidently made by human — I suppose that's the word—human beings. They run from the extremes of ocean bays to the extremes of other ocean bays, and connect, too, the many lakes there. Nature does not make such lines. They are of equal width, those canals, throughout their whole length, and Schiaparelli has even watched them in construction. First there is a dark line, as if the earth had been disturbed, and then it becomes bright when the water is let in. Sometimes, too, double canals are made there close to each other, running side by side, as if one were used for travel and transportation in one direction and one in another. And there are many other things as wonderful. The world of Mars is like our own. There are continents and seas and islands there—it is not a dead, dry surface like the moon—and it has clouds and rains and snows and seasons, just as we have, and of the same intensity as ours. Oh, Julius, we *must* communicate with them!"

"But, my dear, that implies equal interest on their part. How do we know them to be intelligent enough?"

"Why, there are the canals. They must be reasoners in Mars. Besides, how do we know but that they far surpass us in all learning? Mars is much older in one way than the Earth, far more advanced in its planet life, and why should not its people, through countless ages of advantage, have become wiser than we? Whatever their form, they may be superior to us in every way. We are to them, too, something which must have been studied for thousands of years. The Earth, you know, is to the people on Mars a most brilliant object. It is the most glorious object in their sky, a star of the first magnitude. Oh, be sure their astronomers are watching us with all interest!"

And Corbett, dazed, replied that he was overwhelmed with so much learning in one so fair, that he was very proud of her, but that there was one subject on his mind, compared to which communication with Mars or any other planet was but a trifle. And he wanted to talk with her concerning what was closest to his heart. It was the one

great question in the world to him.   It was, when
should be their wedding day?

The girl looked at him blushingly, then paled.
"Let us not talk of that to-day," she said, at
length.   "I know it isn't right; I know that I seem
unkind—but—oh, Julius! come to-morrow and we
will talk about it."   And she began crying.

He could not understand.   Her demeanor was all
incomprehensible to him, but he tried to soothe her,
and told her she had been studying too hard and
that her nerves were not right.   She brightened a
little, but was still distrait.   He left, with something in his heart like a vengeful feeling toward
the planets, and toward Mars in particular.

When Corbett returned next day the girl was in
the library awaiting him.   Her demeanor did not
relieve him.   He feared something indefinable.
She was sad and perplexed of countenance, but
more self-possessed than on the day before.   She
spoke softly: "Now we will talk of what you
wished to yesterday."

He pleaded as a lover will, pleaded for an early
day, and gave a hundred reasons why it should be
so, and she listened to him, not apathetically, but
almost sadly.   When he concluded, she said, very
quietly:

"Did you ever read that queer story by Edmond
About called 'The Man with the Broken Ear'?"

He answered, wonderingly, in the affirmative.

"Well, dear " she said, "do you remember how

absorbed, so that it was a very part of her being, the heroine of that story became in the problem of reviving the splendid mummy? She forgot everything in that, and could not think of marriage until the test was made and its sequel satisfactory. She was not faithless; she was simply helpless.under an irresistible influence. I'm afraid, love"—and here the tears came into her eyes—"that I'm like that heroine. I care for you, but I can think only of the people in Mars. Help me. You are rich. You have a million dollars, and will soon have more. Reach those people!"

He was shocked and disheartened. He pleaded the probable utter impracticability of such an enterprise. He might as well have talked to a statue. It all ended with an outburst on her part.

"Talk with the Martians," said she, "and the next day I will become your wife!"

He left the house a most unhappy man. What could he do? He loved the girl devotedly, but what a task had she given him! Then, later, came other reflections. After all, the end to be attained was a noble one, and he could, in a measure, sympathize with her wild desire. The lover in "The Man With a Broken Ear" had at least occasion for a little jealousy. His own case was not so bad. He could not well be jealous of an entire population of a distant planet. And to what better use could a portion of his wealth be put than in the advancement of science! The idea grew upon him. He would make the trial!

He was rewarded the next day when he told his fiancée what he had decided upon. She was wildly delighted. "I love you more than ever now!" she declared, "and I will work with you and plan with you and aid you all I can. And," she added, roguishly, "remember that it is not all for my sake. If you succeed you will be famous all over the world, and besides there'll come some money back to you. There is the reward of one hundred thousand francs left in 1892 by Madame Guzman to any one who should communicate with the people of another planet."

He responded, of course, that he was impelled to effort only by the thought of hastening a wedding day, and then he went to his office and wrote various letters to various astronomers. His friend Marston, professor of astronomy in the University of Chicago, he visited in person. He was not a laggard, this Julius Corbett, in anything he undertook.

Then there was much work.

Marston, being an astronomer, believed in vast possibilities. Being a man of sense, he could advise. He related to Corbett all that had been suggested in the past for interstellar communication. He told of the suggested advice of making figures in great white roads upon some of Earth's vast plains, but dismissed the idea as too costly and

not the best. "We have a new agent now," he
said. "There is electricity. We must use that.
And the figures must, of course, be geometrical.
Geometry is the same throughout all the worlds
that are or have been or ever will be."

And there was much debate and much corre-
spondence and an exhibition of much learning,
and one day Corbett left Chicago. His destination
was Buenos Ayres, South America.

The Argentine Republic, since its financial
troubles early in the decade, had been in a com-
plaisant and conciliating mood toward all the
world, and Corbett had little difficulty in his first
step—that of securing a concession for stringing
wires in any designs which might suit him upon
the vast pampas of the interior. It was but stipu-
lated that the wires should be raised at intervals,
that herding might not be interfered with. He had
already made a contract with one of the great
electric companies. The illuminated figures were
to be two hundred miles each in their greatest
measurement, and were to be as follows:

It was found advisable, later, to dispense with
the last two, and so, only the square, equilateral
triangle, circle and right-angled triangle, it was
decided should be made. The work was hurried
forward with all the impetus of native energy,

practically unlimited money and the power of love.
This last is a mighty force.

And great works were erected, with vast gener-
ators, and thousands and thousands of miles of
sheets of wires were strung close together, until
each system, when illuminated, would make a
broad band of flame surrounding the defined area.
From the darkened surface of the Earth, at the
time when the Earth approached Mars most nearly,
would blaze out to the Martians the four great geometrical figures. The test was made at last. All
that had been hoped for in the way of an effort
was attained. All along the lines of those great
figures, night in the Argentine Republic was turned
into glorious day. From balloons the spectacle
was something incomparably magnificent. All was
described in a thousand letters. A host of corre-
spondents were there, and accounts of the undertaking and its progress were sent all over the civilized
world. Each night the illumination was renewed,
and all the world waited. Months passed.

Corbett had returned to Chicago. He could do
no more. He could only await the passage of time,
and hope. He was not very buoyant now. His
sweetheart was full of the tenderest regard, but was
in a condition of feverish unrest. He was alarmed
regarding her, so great appeared her anxiety and
so tense the strain upon her nerves. He could not
help her, and prepared to return again to a season
at his mine.

The man was sitting in his room one night in a gloomy frame of mind. What a fool he had been! He had but yielded to a fancy of a dreaming girl, and put her even farther away from him while wasting half a fortune! He would be better on the rugged shore of Lake Superior, where the moods of men were healthy, and where were pure air and the fragrance of the pines. There was a strong pull at his bell.

A telegraph boy entered, and this was on the message he bore:

Come to the observatory at once. Important..

MARSTON.

To seek a cab, to be whirled away at a gallop to the university, to burst into Marston in his citadel, required but little time. The professor was walking up and down excitedly.

"It has come! All the world knows it!" he shouted as Corbett entered, and he grasped him by the hand and wrung it hardly.

"What has come?" gasped the visitor.

"What has come, man! All we had hoped for or dreamed of—and more! Why, look! Look for yourself!"

He dragged Corbett to the eye-piece of the great telescope and made him look. What the man saw made him stagger back, overcome with an emotion which for the moment did not allow him speech. What he saw upon the surface of the planet Mars was a duplication of the glittering figures on the pampas of the South American Republic. They were in lines of glorious light, between what appeared bands of a darker hue, provided, apparently, to make them more distinct, and even at such vast distance, their effect was beautiful. And there was something more, a figure he could not comprehend at first, one not in the line of the others, but above. "What is it—that added outline?" he cried.

"What is it! Look again. You'll determine quickly enough! Study it!" roared out Marston, and Corbett did as he was commanded. Its meaning flashed upon him.

There, just above the representation of the right-angled triangle, shone out, clearly and distinctly, this striking figure:

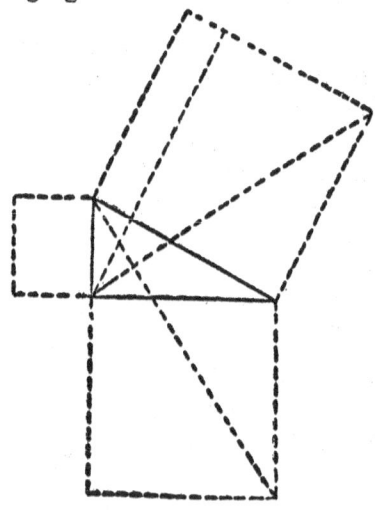

What could it mean? Ah, it required no profound mathematician, no veteran astronomer, to
answer such a question! A schoolboy would be
equal to the task. The man of Mars might have
no physical resemblance to the man of Earth, the
people of Mars might resemble our elephants or
have wings, but the eternal laws of mathematics
and of logic must be the same throughout all
space. Two and two make four, and a straight line
is the shortest distance between two points
throughout the universe. And by adding this
figure to the others represented, the Martians had
said to the people of Earth as plainly as could have
been done in written words of one of our own
languages:

Yes, we understand. We know that you are trying to
communicate with us, or with those upon some other world.
We reply to you, and we show to you that we can reason by
indicating that the square of the hypothenuse of a right-
angled triangle is equivalent to the sum of the squares of the
other two sides. Hope to hear from you further.

There was the right-angled triangle, its lines
reproduced in unbroken brilliancy, and there were
the added lines used in the familiar demonstration,
broken at intervals to indicate their use. The
famous *pons asinorum* had become the bridge
between two worlds.

Corbett could scarcely speak as yet. Telegraph
messengers came rushing in with dispatches
from all quarters—from the universities of Michi-

gan and California, and Yale and Harvard, and from Rochester and all over the United States. Cablegrams from England, France, Germany and Italy and other regions of the world but repeated the same wonderful observation, the same conclusion: "They have answered! We have talked with them!"

Corbett returned to his home in a semi-delirium. He had the wisdom, though it was midnight, to send to Nelly the brief message, "Good news," to prepare her in a degree for what the morning papers would reveal. He slept but fitfully. And it was at an early hour when he called upon his fiancée and found her awaiting him in the library.

She said nothing as he entered, but he had scarcely crossed the threshold when he found his arms full of something very tangible and warm, and pulsing with all love. It has been declared by thoughtful and learned people that there is no sensation in the world more delightful than may be produced by just this means, and Corbett's demeanor under the circumstances was such as to indicate the soundness of the assertion. He was a very happy man.

And she, as soon as she could speak at all, broke out, impulsively:

"Oh, dear, isn't it glorious! I knew you would succeed. And aren't you glad I imposed the hard condition? It was hard, I know, and I seemed unloving, but I believed, and I could not have given you up even if you had failed. I should have told you so very soon. I may confess that now. And— I will marry you any day you wish.''

She blushed magnificently as she concluded, and the face of a pretty women, so suffused, is a pleasing thing to see.

Of course, within a week the name of Corbett became familiar in every corner of the civilized globe, the incentive which had spurred him on became somehow known, and the romance of it but added to his fame, and a few days later, when his wedding occurred, it was chronicled as never had a wedding been before. They made two columns of it even in the far-away Tokio *Gazette*, the Bombay *Times* and the Novgorod *News*. But the social feature was nothing; the scientific world was all aflame.

We had talked with Mars indeed, but of what avail was it if we could not resume the conversation? What next step should be taken in the grand march of knowledge, in the scientific conquest of the universe? Never in all history had there been such a commotion among the learned. Corbett and his gifted wife were early ranked among the eager, for he soon became as much of an enthusiast as she—in fact, since the baby, he is even more so—and derived much happiness from their mutual study and speculation. All theories were advanced from all countries, and suggestions, wise and otherwise, came from thousands of sources.

And so in the year 1900 the thing remains. As inscrutable to us have been the curious symbols appearing upon Mars of late as have apparently been to them a sign language attempted on the pampas. It is now proposed to show to them the outline of a gigantic man, and if Providence has seen fit to make reasoning beings in all worlds something alike, this may prove another bit of progress in the intercourse, but all is in doubt.

Given, the problem of two worlds, millions of miles apart, the people of which are seeking to establish a regular communication with each other, each already acknowledging the efforts of the other, how shall the great feat be accomplished? Will the solution of the vast problem come from a greater utilization of electricity and a further knowledge of what is astral magnetism? There have been, of late, some wonderful revelations along that line. Or will the sign language be worked out upon the planets' surfaces? Who can tell? Certainly all effort has been stimulated, in one world at least. The rewards offered by various governments and individuals now aggregate over five million dollars, and all this money is as nothing to the fame awaiting some one. Who will gain the mighty prize? Who will solve the new problem of the ages?

SCIENCE FICTION

An Arno Press Collection

FICTION

About, Edmond. **The Man with the Broken Ear.** 1872

Allen, Grant. **The British Barbarians:** A Hill-Top Novel. 1895

Arnold, Edwin L. **Lieut. Gullivar Jones:** His Vacation. 1905

Ash, Fenton. **A Trip to Mars.** 1909

Aubrey, Frank. **A Queen of Atlantis.** 1899

Bargone, Charles (Claude Farrere, pseud.). **Useless Hands.** [1926]

Beale, Charles Willing. **The Secret of the Earth.** 1899

Bell, Eric Temple (John Taine, pseud.). **Before the Dawn.** 1934

Benson, Robert Hugh. **Lord of the World.** 1908

Beresford, J. D. **The Hampdenshire Wonder.** 1911

Bradshaw, William R. **The Goddess of Atvatabar.** 1892

Capek, Karel. **Krakatit.** 1925

Chambers, Robert W. **The Gay Rebellion.** 1913

Colomb, P. et al. **The Great War of 189——.** 1893

Cook, William Wallace. **Adrift in the Unknown.** n.d.

Cummings, Ray. **The Man Who Mastered Time.** 1929

[DeMille, James]. **A Strange Manuscript Found in a Copper Cylinder.** 1888

Dixon, Thomas. **The Fall of a Nation:** A Sequel to the Birth of a Nation. 1916

England, George Allan. **The Golden Blight.** 1916

Fawcett, E. Douglas. **Hartmann the Anarchist.** 1893

Flammarion, Camille. **Omega:** The Last Days of the World. 1894

Grant, Robert et al. **The King's Men:** A Tale of To-Morrow. 1884

Grautoff, Ferdinand Heinrich (Parabellum, pseud.). **Banzai!** 1909

Graves, C. L. and E. V. Lucas. **The War of the Wenuses.** 1898

Greer, Tom. **A Modern Daedalus.** [1887]

Griffith, George. **A Honeymoon in Space.** 1901

Grousset, Paschal (A. Laurie, pseud.). **The Conquest of the Moon.** 1894

Haggard, H. Rider. **When the World Shook.** 1919

Hernaman-Johnson, F. **The Polyphemes.** 1906

Hyne, C. J. Cutcliffe. **Empire of the World.** [1910]

In The Future. [1875]

Jane, Fred T. **The Violet Flame.** 1899

Jefferies, Richard. **After London; Or, Wild England.** 1885

Le Queux, William. **The Great White Queen.** [1896]

London, Jack. **The Scarlet Plague.** 1915

Mitchell, John Ames. **Drowsy.** 1917

Morris, Ralph. **The Life and Astonishing Adventures of John Daniel.** 1751

Newcomb, Simon. **His Wisdom The Defender:** A Story. 1900

Paine, Albert Bigelow. **The Great White Way.** 1901

Pendray, Edward (Gawain Edwards, pseud.). **The Earth-Tube.** 1929

Reginald, R. and Douglas Menville. **Ancestral Voices:** An Anthology of Early Science Fiction. 1974

Russell, W. Clark. **The Frozen Pirate.** 2 vols. in 1. 1887

Shiel, M. P. **The Lord of the Sea.** 1901

Symmes, John Cleaves (Captain Adam Seaborn, pseud.). **Symzonia.** 1820

Train, Arthur and Robert W. Wood. **The Man Who Rocked the Earth.** 1915

Waterloo, Stanley. **The Story of Ab:** A Tale of the Time of the Cave Man. 1903

White, Stewart E. and Samuel H. Adams. **The Mystery.** 1907

Wicks, Mark. **To Mars Via the Moon.** 1911

Wright, Sydney Fowler. **Deluge: A Romance** and **Dawn.** 2 vols. in 1. 1928/1929

SCIENCE FICTION

NON-FICTION
Including Bibliographies,
Checklists and Literary Criticism

Aldiss, Brian and Harry Harrison. **SF Horizons.** 2 vols. in 1. 1964/1965

Amis, Kingsley. **New Maps of Hell.** 1960

Barnes, Myra. **Linguistics and Languages in Science Fiction-Fantasy.** 1974

Cockcroft, T. G. L. **Index to the Weird Fiction Magazines.** 2 vols. in 1 1962/1964

Cole, W. R. **A Checklist of Science-Fiction Anthologies.** 1964

Crawford, Joseph H. et al. **"333": A Bibliography of the Science-Fantasy Novel.** 1953

Day, Bradford M. **The Checklist of Fantastic Literature in Paperbound Books.** 1965

Day, Bradford M. **The Supplemental Checklist of Fantastic Literature.** 1963

Gove, Philip Babcock. **The Imaginary Voyage in Prose Fiction.** 1941

Green, Roger Lancelyn. **Into Other Worlds:** Space-Flight in Fiction, From Lucian to Lewis. 1958

Menville, Douglas. **A Historical and Critical Survey of the Science Fiction Film.** 1974

Reginald, R. **Contemporary Science Fiction Authors,** First Edition. 1970

Samuelson, David. **Visions of Tomorow:** Six Journeys from Outer to Inner Space. 1974